Additional books by Matthew F. O'Malley at time of printing Coastside Detectives Changing Tides

Tales for Sale	-2007
Coastside Detectives The Grand View	-2010
Coastside Detectives Armando's Gold	-2012
Tales for Sale II	-2012
Sunsets of Inverness	-2012 (Pen name Joe Ballard)
Coastside Detectives Distant Islands	-2013

COASTSIDE DETECTIVES
CHANGING TIDES

MATTHEW F. O'MALLEY

authorHOUSE°

AuthorHouse™
1663 Liberty Drive
Bloomington, IN 47403
www.authorhouse.com
Phone: 1 (800) 839-8640

Published by AuthorHouse 12/29/2015

ISBN: 978-1-5049-7053-2 (sc)
ISBN: 978-1-5049-7052-5 (e)

Print information available on the last page.

Any people depicted in stock imagery provided by Thinkstock are models,
and such images are being used for illustrative purposes only.
Certain stock imagery © Thinkstock.

This book is printed on acid-free paper.

Because of the dynamic nature of the Internet, any web addresses or links contained in
this book may have changed since publication and may no longer be valid. The views
expressed in this work are solely those of the author and do not necessarily reflect the
views of the publisher, and the publisher hereby disclaims any responsibility for them.

Cover photo by Matthew F. O'Malley.

Back cover author portrait and picture courtesy of Kenney Mencher. To view
more works by Kenney Mencher, please visit Kenney-Mencher.com

Additional information about Coastside Detectives may be found at Coastsided.com

Coastside Detectives Changing Tides is a work of fiction. All characters
and situations described in the book are fictional. Any similarities to
actual persons, events or situations are clearly coincidental.

WEEK I

WEEK 1

1

IT WAS A FRIDAY night in July, and the Surf Spot restaurant complex off Highway One and Fassler Avenue in Pacifica was freshly opened. I had seen signs that the place was open the previous week as I drove up Fassler Avenue on my way to and from home, as the parking lot they shared with Sea Bowl bowling alley was overflowing, but I hadn't been able to arrange a time to drop into the place until after the second week of its opening. That night, I entered through a side fence that had yet to be completed, and took a walk to the restaurant's outdoor dining area in back.

At the time, the place was still a work in progress, with some areas roped off, but you could already see the potential. The beach volleyball pit was filled with sand, but missing a net, the outdoor stage was filled with equipment, and a couple of the cabañas were still off limits, but the rest of the complex was already in place. The fire pits were working, warming lamps were out, the torches that ringed the place were lit, the

1

rolling hills of grass were fresh and bright and green, and the whole place was absolutely packed with smiling people.

Immediately, I located the outside bar and stood in line beneath the fog-gray night sky that reflected the local light of the burning torches back down upon the patrons. Suddenly, I felt the presence of someone standing behind me—too close behind me, even if we were standing in line for alcohol. I turned to ask for some space and found myself looking down upon a woman, approximately four foot five, wearing red flannel pajamas and a hand-knit purple sweater-vest. She had long, thick, tangled gray hair streaked with black that had both colorful and clear beads strung throughout. Large gold dangling earrings were partially concealed in her tresses, and gold and silver bracelets and necklaces were piled upon her in mounds. Her black eyes were wide open as she stood looking up into my face.

"You have a strong aura," she said in a sultry voice.

"Thank you," I replied. "And you have…you have nice jewelry."

"What's your name?" she asked, placing one palm in the air facing just inches from my heart. Her face was aglow from fog and torchlight, and she was breathing heavily.

"Mike. Mike Mason," I said. "And you are?"

"I am Madame Gira," she said, shaking her head as if to cast off some additional energy that was too much for her to handle. "I am a psychic. I can read your aura and predict the future. And I'm an herbalist."

"And an herbalist!" I chuckled.

Madame Gira turned somber as she moved closer and brought her hands up as if to cradle my face. "Oh…" she said as she looked into my eyes. "I see much turmoil in the lives of those around you. Lives are changing. People are changing. Things are coming to light, and not all of them will be for the best."

"Sounds about right," I joked.

"I'm serious." Madame Gira tried to pierce me with a narrowing of her eyes.

"I'm serious too," I replied, but still could not help cracking a smile.

"Oh Mike, Mike," Madame Gira rolled her head clockwise, closed her eyes, and brought her voice down to a deep growl. "You are in danger, Mike Mason," she said, in what was close to a manly voice. "Someone here. Nearby. In this space, wishes to do you great harm. I feel, I feel, I feel…that they wish to have you…murdered!"

I looked around. There wasn't anyone in particular looking at me at the time or looking threatening, although the place was sprawling and the crowd diverse. Anyone filled with ill will could easily have blended in.

"Really!" I said, bemused, as I brought my gaze back to Madame Gira.

"Beware, Mike Mason. Beware!" She continued, "There are dark forces at work around you." Madame Gira brought her hands to my face and began to move them like spiders in the wind. If she was attempting to hypnotize me, it wasn't working, as I was still very much cognizant. She then reached into the back web of her hair and pulled out a purple business card that had shooting stars and a magic wand on it. The card read: Madame Gira—Psychic, Fortune Teller, Herbalist. It also listed her phone number and an address I recognized as the business area in the Manor district of Pacifica.

"Thank you," I said as I placed the card into my breast pocket and patted it. "I'll keep you in mind if I need any herbs." I smiled, then turned toward the walk-up bar and moved up three spaces, not wanting to lose my place to someone cutting in front of me. When I turned back around to continue my conversation with Madame Gira, she had vanished. I scanned the crowd, but somehow she managed to elude me, apparently lost in the crowd.

I checked in with the guy in line ahead of me. "Any drink recommendations?"

He turned, and the look on his face matched the name of the drink he suggested. "A Pisco sour," he said in a thick Slavic accent.

He was a big guy, tall, with broad shoulders. He had some muscle to him, and although he dressed sharply in a black suit, he failed in one respect—he was wearing a thin, white, collared shirt without an undershirt. He was hairy, so much so that his shirt appeared rumpled with all the black hair beneath it. It looked like part of the Amazon forest was lurking beneath a thin veneer of cotton. His thick black hair, wide nostrils on a nose that had the hallmarks of being broken a couple of times being smashed flat and back into his face, and his sloping skull made him look like an Eastern European version of a lowland gorilla.

Another server was added to the bar as we waited, and the line moved. I was now able to scan the bottles on the back wall; many familiar names, some different. Finally, the European gorilla was served, and I was mildly surprised when he turned around and handed me a drink.

"Let this first one be on me." He smiled. "Cheers."

"Cheers." I replied.

I took a small sip, and it immediately didn't sit well.

"No, no, no." He laughed and slapped me on the shoulder. "Like this!" He opened his cavernous mouth and tossed his drink down the well. I tried, but only got half a gulp in me. It just wasn't riding right.

"Ha, ha, ha!" he laughed, then grabbed a trio of drinks and left the line.

Food was now coming to the window and orders were being picked up, so I was asked to wait. As I did, I looked to the crowd to see if I could spot my ape-like friend. I spotted him near the stage, where I watched as he handed a woman and another man their drinks.

That woman looked familiar, but I couldn't quite place her. Her eyes locked with mine, and she quickly looked down and away. The man she was with looked at me then to the man who had brought them their drinks. The profile of the man she was with was that of string bean as he lean leaned forward to speak with the woman. She said something, apparently in reference to me looking at them, and he in turn glanced over at me before being handed the drinks by the guy with the hairy chest, who I decided I would call the Gorilla.

"What're you having?" the bartender asked, pulling my attention to the bar.

"Jameson Manhattan in a bucket of rocks. Splash of water and cherry juice."

"Sure," the bartender said.

I looked back to check on the trio, but they had since moved away from the stage, and as I waited for my whiskey, I took another sip of the Pisco sour the big lug had offered me. It was different, nothing like a whiskey, but now it wasn't as horribly bad as my first two gulps.

"One more moment, sir," the bartender apologized. "Out of cherry juice."

Who was she? I thought to myself as I leaned my back against the bar, waiting for my drink. *Familiar.* I finished off the Pisco sour, paid for and left a tip for my drink, took a cleansing sip of Jameson, and then proceeded to head toward the stage to see if I could locate the trio. That's when I was stopped cold in my tracks, as if I had been struck by a bolt of lightning. That woman was Jessica Windrop.

Jessica Windrop, who had been a secretary at Western Capital Endeavors, the office front of a Ponzi scheme I had brought to the attention of authorities last winter.

Jessica Windrop, the secretary to Darrell Harsher, who died by my gun in an office shootout.

Jessica Windrop, the woman I'd had been searching for the past six months.

Jessica Windrop, the one link I had to another shadowy figure, a figure I knew only as Jasper and who had fronted a hit man to try to take me out.

I dropped my glass and tried to run to where I last saw Jessica and her friends, but my feet wouldn't move. I looked down at my feet that seemed far below me and looked like they stretched for miles into a deep abyss. My world began to spin, everything went fuzzy, then dark, and I felt as if I had been pushed out of an airplane without a parachute. That was the last thing I felt before I apparently hit my head on the cement.

2

WHEN I AWOKE AT the hospital Saturday morning, things were a little fuzzy, and I had a slight headache, but I wasn't going to let the docs know; other than the large bump and growing bruise on my forehead, I was feeling pretty good. Apparently, as I began to fall face forward onto the ground, someone nearby had enough sense and reflexes to partially catch me. After a scan, needles, and a night's rest in the hospital, I found no more reason to stay.

The toxicology reports wouldn't be back for a couple of days, but I was feeling OK and was allowed to leave. I immediately headed to our Coastside Detectives office in Pacifica's Linda Mar shopping center to see if I could dig up anything. It was already late morning when I arrived, so I pulled the blinds, grabbed my chair, pulled open my desk drawer, fished out the bottle of Jameson I keep in there, and poured myself a glass as I turned on my computer. As I waited for it to boot up, I scanned the newspaper headlines of the *Coastal Watch*, paying close attention to the front page stories before jumping to the editorial section to see what my friend Arthur McCoy was reporting. As always, he was predicting the end of civilization, this time as evidenced by a shooting at an old folk's home in San Francisco.

It had been a hectic winter filled with mischief and mayhem; spring and summer had seen our offices becoming a well-oiled machine under the management of a very motivated Marilyn Jackson, our newest paid employee. Under her management, the San Francisco Tenderloin branch of Coastside Detectives was becoming a money-maker, with Marilyn parsing out jobs between Steve Parodi, one of my partners, and Ozzie Ferris, our intern. Steve had been sidelined off and on for months now, spending more time with his ailing mother down in San Diego, so Ozzie was pulled into the Tenderloin branch to take up some of the slack. And Marilyn, once she started getting paid and was no longer an intern herself, began to do outreach to downtown businesses, offering some initial free services to hook the new clients in. Joe Ballard, the senior partner of Coastside Detectives, once skeptical of the offering of free services, quickly changed his mind as new clients started to sign year-long contracts.

With Ozzie having become fully capable in research and background checks, our bread and butter out of our Marina branch, we now began to see similar benefits of his expertise at our Tenderloin office. Money was really flowing in, and all the things that had occupied my time and mind the previous winter had been forgotten. That was until Jessica Windrop had made her unexpected appearance that night at the Surf Spot, and I had been slipped a mickey in my drink by her apparent associate, the man I now called the Gorilla.

Jessica Windrop, who was she? All we knew about her thus far was she had worked at Western Capital Endeavors, a company that had been in the forefront of a Ponzi land scheme run by a two-bit hoodlum known as Darrell Harsher. At the time, I had thought she was just his secretary, but when things unraveled and Darrell was taken out, Jessica mysteriously disappeared into the woodwork and hadn't been seen until last Friday. Joe and I had tried to find her, and had even enlisted Ozzie in trying to track down her history, but all the paths we followed led to dead ends. At some point, I had let her fade out of my memory.

It took five minutes for my computer settle into work mode, and I just began hitting the keys to look up knock drugs when Joe came walking in carrying the type of gun rack you see affixed to the back window of pickup trucks in rural areas. He leaned the rack against my desk and examined the knocks on my head.

"Whoa, what happened to you?"

"Got mickied," I said. "By a friend of Jessica Windrop."

"Jessica…Jessica…you found her?" Joe asked.

"Ran into her. Well not really. Saw her from a distance, recognized her, and that's when the mickied drink her friend had handed to me kicked in."

"What was it?"

"Not sure," I said. "Results aren't in yet."

"You OK? Shouldn't you be home?"

"Naw, I actually feel better sitting up. But hey," I said, changing the subject and pulling my attention away from my mild headache, "what're you doing here on a Saturday?"

"You'll see," Joe said. "Here, give me a hand with this."

I followed Joe as he toted the gun rack to the back of the office, where I found a hammer and some nails and gave him a hand attaching the rack to the back wall.

"What's this all about?" I asked, again trying to figure out what he was up to. "Joe Ballard feng shui?"

"You'll see in a moment," Joe replied.

After the rack was secured to the wall, he went out to his truck and returned, carrying something wrapped in newspaper and with another something strapped to his back. "Here, take these. They're yours," Joe said, presenting me with the package wrapped in newspaper.

I undid the newspaper and found it to be a couple of walking canes.

"Asshole," I said and Joe started laughing. I blew out my knee about a year ago while bike riding, and every so often, it acts up. When that happens, I take to using a walking stick as support. Joe, who is nineteen years my senior, has had great sport of this, referring to me as Old Man whenever I have a flare-up.

"Here," Joe said, reaching out for one the canes that appeared to be made out of bamboo. "Let me see this one." He held the cane by its shaft and pulled the curved handle, revealing it was a sword.

"Nice," I said as he handed it back to me. I swished the sword around in the air, making a Z as Zorro did, and then I carved the letter M through the air. "So what am I supposed to do with this?"

"The same thing you are to do with the other one you are holding, a genuine shillelagh; protect yourself when you're not a hundred percent."

"I'm not going to use these!" I protested.

"Sure you are," Joe said as he grabbed both canes out of my hands, walked over to the back wall, and racked them. "Look, Mike, you're getting to the age where you need extra protection; a crutch, so to speak." Joe was only half joking.

"No I'm not!"

"But wait, get this," he said. "I saved the best for last." Joe unslung the black carrying case he had on his back and handed it over to me.

"What's this?" I asked.

"A Zap Cane," Joe said. "I got it from Heartland America."

I unzipped the carrier and pulled out a black metal cane, the last quarter length of which was absolutely medieval looking, with silver studs and metal straps.

"It's all charged up," Joe said enthusiastically. "And it delivers a powerful million volts, supposedly."

I rolled the cane in my hands. There was an embedded flashlight in the handle and a switch that could be easily pressed. "Did you test it?"

"No," Joe said. "That's what we're going to do now."

"On what?"

"On you," Joe replied.

"No way."

"Aw, come on," Joe said, grabbing it out of my hands. "Don't be such a wuss. We've got to see if it works. I'll just bring it near to you..."

"No way," I repeated, backing up.

"Look. I'll just barely touch you with it."

"No way." I grabbed the cane out of Joe's hands.

"All right then," Joe said. "You just turn it on and touch your leg or something with it. As soon as you start feeling something, you just drop it or pull it away."

I looked warily at Joe but knew he wasn't going to give up on me trying it. I've also seen and heard how rookies in various police academies are often required to be hit or shot by a stun gun before they are allowed to carry one, so it seemed like I had no choice. "All right," I finally agreed after some self-deliberation.

"Let me get behind you, just in case," Joe said as I turned on the cane's switch, first activating the light then the charge at the bottom half of the cane.

"OK," I said, taking a couple of deep breaths. "When I tell you, get ready."

Joe moved up behind me, his hands just inches from either side of me.

"Ready?" I asked.

"Ready," Joe replied.

I took a final deep breath, gritted my teeth, and brought the cane close to my right leg. The shock was immediate, and my right leg shot backward with the electric jolt, kicking Joe away as I fell forward. For the second time in as many of days, I had abruptly made my way to the floor—with very little alcohol.

"You were supposed to have fallen backward," Joe said as he helped me up.

"Couldn't help it," I said, my head now pounding.

"With that kick of yours, you almost made *me* need this to walk," Joe said as he picked the cane up off the floor. "Guess it works well enough, though."

"Oh yeah!" I replied sarcastically. "Good. Almost too good. Could have used this one the other day if I'd known I was going to get mickied by someone. Just walk up, tap their leg, and then bam!"

"Or you know, if someone is giving you trouble and you point it at them, their natural instinct is to grab the end pointing at them. Just think, they'll get it full strength." Both Joe and I reveled in that image before Joe changed the subject.

"Oh, hey, a couple of boys from the Moose Lodge and I are heading up to Donner Lake tomorrow. Rented a cabin for a couple of weeks. Do some fishing, drop down to Carson City and Virginia City for some gambling. Want to go? There's an extra room. Martin dropped out the last minute."

"Naw, it's all right," I said. "Not feeling up to par yet. Especially now. Not sure if the altitude would make things worse."

"Oh, come on," Joe pleaded. "You'd like it. Taking the old Route 40, Lincoln Highway, as it comes in above Donner. Absolutely stunning."

"Ah, can't," I replied. "Really. I'm also having my neighbor over tomorrow. Fixing to have a barbeque."

"New neighbor?" Joe said.

"Old one," I said. "Just Cathy Mays. But maybe next time when you go up to do the lake thing I'll go."

"Sure," Joe said. "Sure."

3

Early Sunday afternoon, I was working my red-topped Coleman barbeque grill, preparing to have a late lunch with my neighbor, Cathy Mays. Cathy had brought over a pitcher of sangria to share, though she was working on finishing it mostly by herself as she sat in my wicker recliner, a glass of sangria in one hand and an overly extended electronic cigarette in the other.

Cathy is an odd bird, a little off, but I like her. She has a sweet heart. She was talking about her latest cruise to the Bahamas. With her hair in a big curly frizz, her large faux pearl necklace and bracelets, and overly tanned skin adding ten years to her age, she looked like she was the illegitimate daughter of comedian Phyllis Diller and Mrs. Roper from *Three's Company*. She also has a little dog named Rover. I take him out for her and watch him now and again when she's away.

When the coals were hot enough, I placed a can of beans, a can of creamed corn, and a bread pan containing the meatloaf I'd purchased from the Fresh and Easy over at San Pedro Point on the grill. I turned on the patio radio, and a block of Creedence Clearwater Revival came on.

"Oh, I just love these guys," Cathy said in a raspy voice. "They really knew how to groove back then." She put down her drink, put her cigarette in her mouth, and began to snap her fingers to the music as she danced in her chair, looking much like the Penguin out of the *Batman* television show from the sixties.

As always when I'm around Cathy, I try not to look too closely at her mouth when she talks due to her deep under bite. I keep my eyes averted or darting around her and sometimes I wonder if she thinks I'm just shy or something. I find it even more disturbing when she drinks, as her lower jaw extends and her teeth clink against her glass. Being unsure of her dental capabilities, what I was cooking was something I hoped she could get through with little problems, hence the meatloaf and creamed corn.

Poseidon, my orange tabby, had decided to join our barbecue as soon as he heard me close the grill. He now sat in rapt attention before Cathy, as if every word that came from her mouth contained a piece of golden kibble, which maybe it did.

"Your cat scares me," Cathy finally said when she took notice of Poseidon sitting at her feet. She took a long drag on her electronic cigarette, the vapor erupting from her nostrils and over her lips like some lahar. She then took another swig of her glass of sangria and washed it down with another deep drag on her cigarette.

Poseidon, in apparent acknowledgement that we were talking about him, jumped onto the table next to Cathy and tried to swat at the electronic fog she expelled in a cough.

"Shoo," Cathy said to Poseidon. "Come on, shoo."

Poseidon turned his back to her and remained on the table.

"Come on Poseidon. Down," I commanded and Poseidon responded by jumping off the table, walking around me once, embracing me with his tail as he went, then finding a comfortable spot on the deck, where he could close his eyes as he looked toward the sun or open them when he needed to check in on Cathy.

"You know those electronic cigarettes are probably just as bad as the real ones," I said.

"Until they have scientific proof, I won't worry about it," Cathy said as she refilled her glass of sangria.

"Here, here!" I toasted. "Ignorance is bliss." Just then, my cell phone began to buzz. It was the alarm system going off at our Tenderloin office. We had been hit at all of our offices a while back, and it looked like we were getting hit again.

"Be right back," I said to Cathy as I ran into my house and up the stairs to my home office; Poseidon was on my heels to see what all the fuss was about.

I hopped onto my computer and pulled up our Tenderloin office's hidden security cameras. I could see someone was indeed inside our office, but couldn't make out his face as he was wearing a hoodie. I could also see he had disabled the security cameras we had left out in the open, but didn't find our hidden cameras. These pinhole hidden security cameras are virtually invisible to the naked eye, but being that size also limits their image quality. There was no sound, but it appeared this perp had somehow disabled the primary alarm system we had installed, but not the secondary hidden one that had alerted me of the break-in.

I could see this gloved intruder had brought in a box and placed it on a desk. Within that box were a couple of cans of spray paint and some tools, including a small crowbar, a hammer, and possibly a hacksaw.

He was taking his time as he went to work, almost lackadaisical as he moved around the place.

I went to my office closet, pulled out a coat, looked back at the computer screen, and saw Hoodie just as he looked up from digging in one of the desks. He then headed for the box, grabbed the crowbar from it, and headed toward the back office. Someone's arm, stretching out of the back office doorway, entered my view and was handed the crowbar.

So there were at least two of them. I went to my bedroom and grabbed my gun from my dresser. When I returned to my office, Poseidon had already made himself comfortable on my keyboard.

"Poseidon!" I yelled and tossed him to the floor, but it was too late, there were some error messages on my screen. I hit a couple of keys, but to no avail. I couldn't get anywhere and would need to reboot, but it was already getting late. I had to make a dash to the office before the burglars were gone.

"Gotta go!" I yelled to Cathy as I ran out the back gate. "There's a break-in at one of my offices. We'll have to do this again! Have another barbeque sometime!" I hopped into my dark purple Pontiac Bonneville and rushed to our Tenderloin office.

Having the break-ins last winter afforded us the opportunity to upgrade our computers and network. With Ozzie's expertise, we had purchased a couple of fast servers at all of our offices and networked them out of our Pacifica office. We put cages around them, vented them, and secured them so that it'd take a 900 pound gorilla to steal them. The Gorilla—as I drove, the thought came to mind that maybe my being mickied by the Gorilla and this new break-in were connected; but then again, maybe not. Just a coincidence, I convinced myself. More likely, this latest break-in was probably being performed by the same guys who had hit us about a year ago. Many times when you are hit, the same ones will hit you again a few months later, after you've replaced everything; a second chance to score some now new merchandise. And if these were the same guys, they would probably be there for a while. Last time, it looked as if they had spent a good deal of time just trashing our office, spray painting the walls and uprooting the potted plants. Based upon the contents of the box they had brought in, the one containing a few cans of spray paint, they were planning to do the same again.

As I drove, I thought about whom I should call for backup. I could call the police, but they would probably show up late and allow the criminals to get away, or if they did capture the burglars, they would be kept out of my hands and I would never get a chance to glean any information as to the full scope and purpose of their activities. Stealing was one thing, but the damage they had previously done, the way things had been turned upside down in our offices, in the previous break-ins gave me doubts that their intentions were strictly for cash.

I also thought about calling Joe, but he was too far away, up at Donner Lake at the California and Nevada border, while Steve Parodi was in San Diego, near the Mexico border. Ozzie, our tech genius, couldn't intimidate a fly, and Marilyn, ah, I couldn't call her. Though she is street smart, I still wasn't sure how she would handle herself in a shaky situation.

No, I was going to have to do this on my own. I pulled up near the Tenderloin police station, a few buildings down from our office. There were a couple of Safeway shopping carts outside our office and one of them had a computer in it. There were a couple of homeless drug dealing fellas I recognized outside. They had been attracted to our front door, sensing an opportunity might arise for them to take part in a feeding frenzy. That pissed me straight off. As pushed my way through, these destitute denizens scattered, and I charged into my office, gun drawn.

"Freeze, asshole!" I yelled at a thin black guy who was at the box of tools the thieves had brought in. He was holding a hacksaw in one hand and had his other hand in the box. It was the same guy who I had seen wearing a hoodie on my computer thirty minutes earlier, and I knew him. It was a guy I had caught a couple of years ago pissing on our front door. I had run him off back then and hadn't seen him since. I guess he had forgotten what had happened to him last time. I stepped in closer to this guy, gun pointing at his forehead. When he saw me, he was again having an issue as to when it was an appropriate time to relieve himself.

I dropped low behind a desk, my gun still trained on the Pisser. There was still someone not accounted for, the guy in the back, so after a moment during which I heard a little movement, I yelled, "You in the back office. Come on out. I know you're back there."

There was silence for a beat, and then the sound of footsteps as someone made their way to the back office doorway; it was guy I had seen in the back. He was also wearing a hoodie. I couldn't see him clearly due to the shadow on his face created by his hood and the Pisser standing in front of him, so I barked out some orders. "You, with the hacksaw, put it down, raise your hands in the air, and sit down over in that chair. Keep your hands up where I can see them. *Sit down!*" I barked at the Pisser. Having him sit in a chair would delay him from making any sudden movements in my direction as I worked on getting his buddy squared away. The Pisser complied and sat in a chair. "Legs crossed." I added and he followed my orders to a 'T'.

And you…" I began to direct orders to the one in the back doorway, but instead, I watched as he unzipped his jacket to expose a thin frame. He then pulled back his hood.

At first I didn't recognize him, but when I did, I at first thought Steve Parodi had driven up from San Diego and had come upon our place being burglarized. But no, it wasn't that—Steve was both burglarizing and trashing our place. A smile crossed his face when he realized I had finally recognized him.

I stood up from where I had been crouching, walked over to the guy in the chair, the Pisser, and crouched down behind him. I let him feel the cold barrel of my gun against his ear and cheek as I whispered in his other ear, keeping my eyes on Steve.

"I want you to get up slowly and then head out that door." He immediately began to move, but I stayed him with a forceful hand on his shoulder. "And this time, I want you to remember, if I ever see you again in this building, on this block, in this neighborhood, that's it. Get it? No more chances."

The Pisser stood up and quickly headed out the front door. I then motioned with the barrel of my gun for Steve to take the now vacant seat. I moved to the doorway, glanced into the back room to ensure it was vacant. It was, but trashed. I found another seat across from Steve and looked him over. It wasn't the same Steve who had started with us. It wasn't even the same Steve I had seen a few months earlier. He was gaunt, thin, ashy, and pockmarked. He looked absolutely ugly, sporting a Dead Milkmen T-shirt.

"I thought you were in San Diego," I began, still attempting to come to terms with the situation I found myself in. "What are you doing running around with that crackhead?" I said in reference to the Pisser.

Steve lowered his gaze and I finally took a moment to look around the office. Just like the last time we were hit, the place was a disaster. The walls had been spray painted with long lines, and as before, Marilyn's paintings had been shredded. The plants had been pulled from the pots and tossed around the room. The files from the filing cabinets had been tossed in the air, and boxes had been emptied. All of the drawers on the desks had been opened and the contents rifled through. The only difference between this and the last time was that most of the computers were still on the desks. We had locked them down with cables. They had apparently cut through one of them, the one in the shopping cart outside the office, but it most surely had slowed their progress in getting any of the others.

"Why Steve?" I finally asked. "Why?"

"I needed money," Steve said.

"Money?" I asked, then, "Money! All you needed to do was ask. But this…this…I just don't get it."

I looked at Steve's hands. They were still gloved, but I also noticed they were twitching. I could also see he had at least taken part in the spray painting of the office, as his gloves were speckled with red drops of paint. He was still keeping his eyes down, not looking at me, but I knew how to get his attention.

"Take off your hoodie," I said, and Steve slowly looked me in the eyes.

"Take off your hoodie!" I demanded. "Let me see your arms."

"Fuck you," he said.

I got out of my chair, cocked my gun toting arm in preparation for hitting him, and threatened one last time, "Do what I say before, God help me, you make me regret what will happen next!"

Steve looked into my eyes, saw the fury inside of me, and then attempted to take off his gloves, nonchalantly first pulling at the fingertips before resorting to biting the tip with his teeth and pulling them off. His teeth were rotten, falling out, and even from where I stood, I could smell the decay.

Steve dawdled when it came to removing his jacket. He was trying to show that he was in control by taking off his gloves, something I hadn't asked him to do. I'd let him have his little victory, but I reminded him who held the cards.

"Jacket. Now!" I commanded.

Steve took his time, apparently struggling to take off his hoodie, but after he had tossed his jacket into a pile onto the desk next to his gloves, he quickly folded his arms. I grabbed one of his arms and extended it, then realized his struggling and apparent defiance had been just a delay tactic over a source of embarrassment advertised on his arms: red streaks, infections, and drug scars.

I swore under my breath.

Steve, the shy one.

Steve, the innocent one.

Steve, the young guy who I was to take under my wing, my protégé.

Steve, the young guy who helped to expand our offices

Steve, our partner.

Steve, the drug addict.

Steve was like family—office, business family. All of this, the damage, he didn't need to do this. And the only reason I could think why he would do this, this damage, the graffiti, the ripping out of the plants, was that he must have felt betrayed. This was revenge, this was anger, this was...this was my fault. I had to choke back the overwhelming sadness I was feeling, knowing I had to take responsibility and control for Steve's sake. Steve was pouting and I let his arm fall onto his lap.

"Look. I'm sorry I didn't look out for you more," I said. I put my gun in the back of my waistband as I began to pace. "That's my fault. But I'll make amends. We'll find you some sort of rehab facility, get you cleaned up. Get you back onto the straight and narrow. I'll go with you to the meetings, whatever you need. Joe will help out as well, I'm sure of it. Don't worry; we'll get through this together."

I could see it in Steve's eyes; the rims were watering. I had made some sort of breakthrough to him. He was a good guy, just led astray by this decrepit neighborhood and a boss who hadn't paid him enough attention. Now I knew what Marilyn had meant when she'd said months ago that these white boys I was hiring were greener than grass.

"Yeah, that's what we'll do," I said. "We'll get you straightened up in no time. And you know Joe. Joe, of course, will be fully into it. Yeah, we'll get you someplace, someplace outta here, maybe that Mountain Vista rehab center always advertised on television. You know the one, out in Napa County."

"I gotta tell you something," Steve mumbled, but I was on a roll.

"Yeah, clean air, safe and secluded. That's what you need. Someplace totally different and away from here, and then…and then, well, we'll figure something out. We'll get a plan together as to where you can go next."

"I need to confess something to you," Steve said, this time loud enough to grab my attention.

"Yeah, what is it?" I stopped pacing to look at him squarely.

"A while back…" Steve looked up and saw that he had my attention, then he looked back to where his hands were picking loose skin off his fingers.

"A while back," he repeated, "I don't know, maybe six months ago, this guy came up to me. Met him over on Jessie Street, near Sixth. He offered me a roll of bills if I would let him bug our offices."

I felt my mouth drop open. "Shit," I said.

"I didn't let him, Mike. He wanted to, but I didn't let him."

"That's good," I said, feeling a sense of relief. "That's very good, Steve." I tried not to sound like it, but at the moment, I felt I was almost talking baby talk to him.

"Then he came around again, and again. He kept showing up around the area, in different places. Wherever I went, he would eventually show up. He would show up, and he would intimidate all of my contacts. Anyone I met would soon tell me of their encounters with this guy, and then they would either disappear or avoid me."

"When you say contacts, you mean your dealers?"

"No, anyone I regularly met. God, even the guy at the liquor store wouldn't let me in his place anymore. Everyone is afraid."

"Well who is he? Describe him to me."

Steve rubbed his head. "Well, he's big, wide. Washboard ridges on his forehead and flat nose. He has brown eyes and he is always, always wearing a black suit and tie."

A chill went down my spine. "Does he sound Slavic? Sort of looks like a gorilla, a big hairy chested guy?"

"Yeah. That's him," Steve said. "I think we are talking about the same guy. You know him?"

"Met him before," I replied.

"Then you know he's persistent," Steve said, rubbing his arms. "He kept coming back. Showing up. After me. Making my life a living hell, until one day, when I needed something from one of my regular contacts and he was missing."

"Who was missing? The Gorilla or your drug dealer?" I said drug dealer so Steve had to face it. Like an alcoholic, the first step is to admit you have a problem.

"Both," Steve said without flinching. "I stopped seeing the Gorilla and my contact..."

"Dealer," I corrected him, and he swallowed hard.

"Dealer," Steve admitted. "Was gone. The word on the street was my contact…my dealer…had been chopped up. Freaking literally chopped up!"

"If anything makes you want to stay away from drugs and that life, I think that would be a good sign."

"You don't understand, Mike." Steve started to rub his arms, up and down the track marks. "Mike, you can't understand unless you've tried it. You must have it. There's no thought process, no prompting, no nothing that will stop the urge. You must have it. I can't stop, Mike, I can't. I need it. I want it."

"It sounds like it was a while back when your dealer disappeared. How long ago was that? What did you do to get you where you are now?"

"God, I don't know. It was months back. I don't know anymore. I just went around and no one would sell me anything. I asked everyone and anyone. I even asked some of my cop friends if they knew anything and they all came back with the same. They said the word on the streets was that I was off limits."

"No drugs?"

"Nothing. I was at the end of my rope, Mike. You got to believe me. I couldn't do anything else. I had to ask around for him."

"The Gorilla."

"The Gorilla," Steve confirmed. "And there he suddenly was, and he gave me what I needed, Mike. Mike, I wasn't in control. I didn't ask for this to happen to me. I didn't. He never ever asked for any money, and he never ever asked me to do anything until…" Steve stopped in midsentence. "I probably shouldn't tell you."

I had been slowly getting mad at Steve as he recounted his failings and his dealings with the Gorilla, but when he paused in recounting what had been happening recently, I was barely able to conceal my anger. "What did he ask you to do?"

"He didn't offer me money," Steve said, as if that would lessen the impact of what he would say next. "He just gave me a thumb drive. Told me to run an application on it on a computer and tell him when it was done."

I shook. I literally shook. "And you thought nothing of it?"

Steve could see my anger and I knew he was about to clam up, so I reined myself in.

"Which computer?" I asked, knowing Steve had done as instructed.

"That one." Steve pointed to the computer on the front desk.

"And then what?"

"When I returned it to him, telling him I did as instructed, he had some guys beat me. He didn't even give me anything for doing what he said to do!"

"So basically, you bugged or sabotaged or did something to one of our computers, and what *you* thought would be your promised reward, drugs, didn't come through. And since you didn't get your drugs, you've been clean ever since. Correct?"

"Oh no. That part is OK now. The people I hang out with, my contacts, we're all good again now."

"Good again. All good again now," I repeated as I rubbed my face with my hands and then looked once again around the room. Our office was totally trashed. The walls were spray painted and plants had again been pulled from their pots and tossed around the room. Files had been rifled through and tossed into the air. "Then what do you call this?" I asked. "What do you call this trashing of our office?"

"I needed money," Steve said.

"You needed money. Did you need to trash the place as you got it?"

"I needed to cover my tracks. So you wouldn't catch on."

"And you did it before, the other times at our other offices."

Steve didn't say a thing, and I just blew up. "This is fucking over the top!" I screamed. "Marilyn is going to have a heart attack!"

"Marilyn." Steve spat on the floor, and I slapped him.

"You always liked her more than me." Steve cried, "You and Joe are grooming her to be above me. You already gave her more responsibilities; is she going to be a partner now? Are you going to have me report to her?"

I now knew where Steve's misdirected anger toward us originated. As Steve slowly had been falling by the wayside from his deeper dependence on drugs, our increasing dependence and appreciation of Marilyn's work was eclipsing our initial admiration of, and aspirations for Steve. He was a shadow of his former bright-eyed self, and he blamed Marilyn and us for his problems, not his dependence on drugs.

Drugs and the Tenderloin. I once heard that the Tenderloin was a place of containment. Police, local politicians, they all knew that drugs, prostitution, and any other sort of vice occurs in the area, and they strove to not eradicate or wipe it out, but just to contain it to this one part of the city, where it was a free-for-all. Steve was now in it, fully, and he wouldn't get out. He was contained, and in that part of his life, he was quite content.

"OK," I said. "Where's your gun? I need you to hand it over."

"I don't have it," Steve responded. "Haven't had it for a long time."

"You lost it? Where the fuck is it?"

"Yeah, I lost it. I don't know where it is now."

"You sold it for some drugs, didn't you?"

Steve didn't answer. He was probably ashamed that it was the truth. He just sat there in that stupid Dead Milkmen T-shirt, with his pockmarked face, failing teeth, and tracks on his arms, and shrugged his shoulders.

Staring at him, I was getting swept up in a range of emotions. I felt sorry for Steve. He was now a slave to drugs. I also felt remorse for his life and my failure to guide him. I was frightened about what could have been loaded on that computer and what was most likely being stolen from us or delved into; information on all of our clients, information on us, financials, personal, and business. My emotions took a final turn. I was pissed. I was pissed at the Gorilla, what was happening, and now also disappointed in Steve for not having the willpower and fortitude to conquer his own internal demons, as well as the position he now left me in. And on top of all of that, another gun was on the street, another round of bullets waiting to be used in some crime.

"Get the fuck out of here!" I said. "I can't even stand to look at you."

Steve rose from his chair slowly. He grabbed his hoodie and gloves and slunk toward the door.

"You heard what I said to your bunky?" I yelled after him. "I don't want to see you here anymore, either. And if I do, that's it!"

Steve opened the door and left without saying a word. I followed him to close the door. The computer that had been in the shopping cart was gone, taken by any number of people. I closed the door and surveyed the damage again. On the side wall, just above Marilyn's desk, there was a scribble of spray paint that read, *New paint won't get rid of me*.

No, I thought. New paint didn't get rid of you, but I just did.

4

"O<small>ZZIE! WHERE YOU AT</small>?" I was becoming frantic. After Steve left, I started to freak out about whatever had been installed on that computer; what it was doing, what it was still doing.

"Don't touch anything on any of those computers," Ozzie said after I explained the situation. "I'll be right over."

I began to clean up, stacking the files into piles, sweeping, and putting plants back into their respective pots. Every so often, though, I found myself looking over at the computer that had been compromised as if it might get up and start walking around the room or something. When I got around to Marilyn's desk, I found she had been working on the Thomas Ballard file again. Thomas Ballard was Joe's father, who had started the Coastside Detectives business back in 1935. He had been murdered sometime in the 1970s, and the case remained unsolved. Marilyn had taken this file as a personal mission to see if there was anything she could do to help close the case. As I collated her notes the best I could back into the manila folder, I found a list of names she had handwritten on a piece of steno notebook paper:

Thomas Ballard	-	(Father, PI)
Joe Ballard	-	(Son)
Frank Mason	-	(Officer, Father)
Mike Mason	-	(Son)
James Callahan	-	(Officer, Frank's partner)
Brian Maloney	-	(Reporting Officer)
Roosevelt Jones	-	(Witness?)

Most of the names were of course familiar to me, as I had looked into the file before and had read the newspaper and police reports. Thomas Ballard was Joe's father, Frank was my dad, and James was my dad's partner. Frank and James had come across the body of Thomas Ballard on Burritt Street, an alleyway above the Stockton Tunnel, and had reported it to their police captain, Brian Maloney. As for the last name Marilyn had written down, Roosevelt Jones, I remember him being a possible witness but shortly after the police investigation began, he disappeared.

I checked the rest of Marilyn's notes, but just found doodles of triangles, arrows, squares, a happy face, a sad face, a flower, a car, and a shooting gun. It looked like doodles someone makes when on the phone or pondering something while supposedly listening to someone talk. I was definitely going to follow up with her when I had a chance. I closed the file, put it in her top desk drawer, and continued cleaning up the office during the more than an hour it took Ozzie to arrive.

"Holy Crap!" Ozzie cursed when he came into the office, a computer bag slung over his shoulder. "He really did a number on this place."

"Not as bad as last time," I said.

"Whatcha mean?"

"Remember when we were hit last year, all of our offices?" Ozzie nodded.

"Well Steve was the one who hit this and the Marina office."

"Really?!" Ozzie's eyes widened, and then he shook his head and said, "So which PC do you want me to look at?"

"This one over here." I guided Ozzie to the computer at the front desk.

"He did it to just this one?" Ozzie asked.

"I don't know," I replied. "Steve said just one, but I don't trust it. Maybe he did something to the PCs in all of the offices."

"Or all of them got infected after this one." Ozzie laid his computer bag down and was about to punch some of the keys on the keyboard, but he stayed his hands. "Why would he knowingly infect a computer?" Ozzie asked.

"Someone instructed him to do so," I replied.

"So this is probably some serious stuff going on here."

"Yes."

"How serious?"

"Very."

"OK," Ozzie said. "Just to take over abundance of precaution, let's make it look like we just had some sort of power failure. I'll go to the server and hard drop the power, and when I do so, you just go around and unplugged all of the computers. Start with this one first. Got it?"

"Got it."

Ozzie went into the back office, got into our server cage, and then hollered as he powered down the server. I unplugged the computers. When he was done and all of the computers were turned off, he closed the server cage and met me at the suspect desktop.

He unplugged the network cable, powered up the computer while holding down some keys on the keyboard, and began sniffing around. He pulled a note pad and pencil from his breast pocket. Although a computer guy, Ozzie still used pencils. After an hour, I could tell he was beginning to get frustrated.

"Anything?" I asked for the umpteenth time.

"This one is sophisticated," he said. "May take time. Whatever this program is, I think it spread."

I stood up straight. "You mean all of these computers are infected?"

"Maybe," he said. "Or maybe it's on one of our servers, or hidden somewhere on our network, on our router. It's hard to tell. Wherever it is, it's going to take some time to find it."

"Can you tell what it's doing?"

"Not yet. And actually, it can be doing just about anything. It can be recording every keystroke, learning user names and passwords, it can be replicating all of the files elsewhere, it can be using our computers and servers as a base to attack somewhere else. It's too early to tell yet."

As always what happens to me when I start talking computer hacking with Ozzie, I became paranoid. "Have you found out what they could have been after, what they are getting?"

"Not yet. How long ago do you think the PC got infected?"

"Steve said approximately six months, but who knows?"

"Well, the damage has already been done on whatever was already on the computers and server. Already replicated, if that is what was done. It's new stuff, current right now new activity that we should worry about." Ozzie shut the computer down, inserted a thumb drive and an external hard drive, and rebooted the PC.

"What are you doing now?" I asked.

"I'm going to clone the PC. I want to make sure no one knows we're onto them. Once I have it cloned, we'll try cleaning up the copy and see what we find. This might take a bit to copy."

I left Ozzie alone and went back to work cleaning up the office. *Poor Marilyn*, I thought to myself, *she's going to freak when she sees her paintings ripped to shreds.* After about an hour, Ozzie signaled that the copy was complete as he shut down the infected PC. He then connected the external hard drive that was a copy of the infected PC to the laptop he had brought in. He ran some programs and diagnostics on the copied data.

"Sir-hacks-a-lot?" I said, amused by one of Ozzie's user names.

"On my free time," Ozzie assured me. "In order to fight the enemy, you have to know your enemy. Oh, whoa...what's this?"

"What's what?" I asked.

Ozzie didn't reply. He just started quickly typing on his keyboard. "Whoa. Whoa!" he repeated.

"What?!" I yelled. "What's going on?!"

"One moment," Ozzie said. He pulled his pencil off the desk and clenched it in his teeth as he typed frantically for a few more moments before jerking the external hard drive cord from his laptop. He then began to type wildly on his computer, laughing though his clenched teeth and pencil.

"What's so funny?" I asked as Ozzie's laptop screen turned to blue just before it shut down.

"That was a good one. A good one," Ozzie said, leaning back in his chair and taking the pencil out of his mouth. "Got me good on that one."

"What?" I asked.

"This little virus, or hack, or whatever you want to call it that was on that desktop over there has a self-destruct button or code within

35

it. My testing or snooping activated it. At first I saw it at work on the external hard drive; everything was getting encrypted and then deleted. So I first tried to stop it, then I tried to disconnect it logically from my laptop. When I could see it was beginning to infect my laptop, I physically disconnected the hard drive, but by then it was already too late."

"So your laptop is dead?"

"Toast."

"Think you'll be able to retrieve the data? I heard no matter how much you try to delete something on a computer, there are ways to get to that data."

"There are ways to do that, but this data was encrypted first, and then deleted. There is no way to unencrypt the data unless you have a key. Like I said, a good one."

"So now what?"

"I'll take home the desktop. Work from there. I've got some tricks up my sleeve. I'll figure this one out."

I unlocked the desktop as Ozzie unplugged the cables from the monitor, mouse, and keyboard. "I guess you're right," Ozzie said. "This one is serious. But I'll have some answers soon. I know some people."

I escorted Ozzie to his little green Smart Fortwo coup and placed the desktop on the seat next to him.

"Damn!" Ozzie said, shaking his head. "I still can't get over Steve."

"Me either," I said, and followed with, "Stay out of trouble."

"You too!" Ozzie said. "I'll hook up with you tomorrow over here. I'm now worried about our servers at all of the offices. Remember not to turn anything on until I get in."

I walked back to the office and thought about calling Joe, but it was already ten in the evening. I decided to wait until late the next morning to fill him in. He was on vacation.

WEEK II

5

THE NEXT MORNING, I received a frantic call from Marilyn. "Mike, we've been broken into! There's spray paint everywhere, and the place has been trashed."

"Yeah, there was something going on over the weekend," I replied. "Alarms went off, and I caught some people in the act. Maybe you didn't notice yet, but I did try to clean up a little."

I didn't want to tell Marilyn right off that it was Steve who had trashed the place because with her paintings shredded, it seemed some of Steve's anger was directed at her. I also still felt I needed to protect him a little.

"I was wondering," Marilyn said. "I saw that someone had been sweeping. I thought that was a little strange."

"I also had Ozzie pull one of our computers to see if it had been hacked. Another PC had been stolen. He'll be coming back in around noon. Hold tight and I'll catch up with you in a bit."

I grabbed a coffee and a bagel at the P-Town Café as I made my way to the Tenderloin. Even though the Tenderloin is in the heart of the city, a good cup of coffee is hard to come by. When I reached the office, I found Marilyn had been busy cleaning some more, and Ozzie was hard at work, typing, pausing, then typing again on his keyboard.

"Find anything?" I asked.

"Did I ever!" Ozzie said. "I found the Trojan virus. It moved from the computer to our servers, then to a place on our routers. So check this out. There was this program loaded on our first PC, the one you mentioned Steve had compromised..."

"Steve?" Marilyn said in shock.

I waved her off, and Ozzie continued, "So basically, this program uses this PC to establish a secure tunnel to transfer information from our IP address to somewhere else."

"What information, what kind of stuff, and to where?"

"I'm still working on that, and have some friends who are doing the same. But what this program also does is it propagates to every device on our network, including our router, and for all I can tell, all the way out to our Internet connection. It's a virus. It finds a machine, infects it, and makes itself at home to do whatever is requested of it."

"And that is?"

"I've been monitoring what it does. It seems to scan the hard drive of the device it has infected, and then transmits whatever it finds elsewhere. It also has a real-time component in that it records keystrokes, basically stealing your passwords or whatever you type in, and sends all of that to wherever. The third component is that after it looks for uninfected devices on the network and attempts—well, actually successfully does infect that one, it sets up a complicated auto self-destruct command where it encrypts the hard drive and then wipes it clean if need be. That way, it's very hard to retrieve the lost data.

Fortunately, it appears there is some bug in the code of the self-destruct portion of the command, and it sometimes doesn't run even if tripped."

"Can you stop it—completely disable it, the whole shebang?"

"I did that already at our Marina branch, with this," Ozzie held up a thumb drive. "It's a little application some friends and I created a while back. I like to think of them as little spiders. They'll crawl all over your network and kill whatever you have programmed them to kill."

"And you're sure it will work?"

"It worked over at the Marina branch," Ozzie insisted. "It will kill it, but won't prevent a device from getting infected again. But once installed, it will continue to scan whatever device and network we have it installed on, and if it finds that application again, it will immediately kill it. All I have to do is to insert it in and…"

"Hold off." I stopped Ozzie from inserting the drive into the USB port on the computer. "If we clear the bug, will we be able to monitor their activities if we stop them from monitoring our activity?"

"No, we won't be able to monitor their activity, since the bug will be dead, and they won't be able to monitor our stuff."

"OK," I said. "Then let's hold off. I know you've already cleared our Marina office, but let's leave this alone until we find more information, like where all of this stuff is being sent."

"Gotcha," Ozzie said. "My buddies should have some info for us in a little bit."

"OK, now what's this about Steve?" Marilyn had been getting increasingly antsy while I'd been working with Ozzie, and she finally burst.

"Steve was the one who trashed our offices," I said. Then I continued with, "Look, I don't want you to think this was in any way directed at you."

"Not directed at me?" Marilyn said. "Oh come on, Mike. Look at what he did. You can't tell me he wasn't attacking me, tearing up my paintings. That was all against me."

"Well, OK. Steve does have some issues with you, but really, I think it's all about drugs..."

"Oh no, it ain't," Marilyn countered. "This hacking, putting something on our network, that's not about drugs. This is something else. And he didn't need to put something on our PCs. All he had to do is copy whatever he wanted onto an external hard drive. He knows the passwords to most of our stuff. Someone else wanted to know our business. What's this all about?"

Ozzie looked up from his computer. He wanted to know, too, so I laid it out the best I could with what I had figured out so far.

"I guess it all started a couple of years ago, with Laura. Laura Grandviewer."

"Who?" Ozzie asked.

"A client of ours from a few years ago. Anyway, she was tied up in an international smuggling ring, and well, one thing led to another, and Joe and I had to take her out."

"You mean?" Ozzie ran a finger across his throat.

"Not in that way," I assured them. "There was a gun battle, she took shots at us, and we countered. It wasn't what we wanted to do. And then about a year later, something else happened, and some other people died in the park."

"You mean over in San Pedro County Park!" Ozzie laughed. "You practically almost brought down the mountainside! Did they ever forgive you for that?"

I couldn't help but smirk. "No. Still banned from the park." Then I grew solemn. "There were a number of people who died at that time, murders and whatnot. At the time, I thought what happened at the park ended things right there."

"So you think this first one, this Laura Grandviewer, and the incident at San Pedro are connected?" Marilyn asked.

"Think so? Know so. Joe and I learned that fact just last year, with the Western Capital Endeavors case. Both of you remember that one, don't you?"

They nodded in agreement. "Well, what Joe and I didn't tell you, and what was kept out of the papers, was that there was this Frank Switch fellow, the one I got into a shootout with over at Skyline College. He was a hit man who was sponsored by someone with ties to both Laura Grandviewer and the people who died in San Pedro County Park."

"So you think this same person is the one who hacked us or put this virus or whatever it is onto our computers," Marilyn stated.

"I thought about it and that it makes the most logical sense to me, but it's not necessarily who put Steve up to compromising our computer network. The guy he said told him to do it was this big guy I'm calling the Gorilla, and I just don't take him as the guy behind the curtain. There is someone else pulling the strings."

"Who?" Marilyn asked the question for all of us.

"Million dollar question," I replied. I let Ozzie and Marilyn ponder these revelations for a few moments before I asked Marilyn about something that had been bugging me since I first saw it.

"So Marilyn, while I was cleaning up this mess over the weekend, I came across one of your notebooks with my name and my father's name. Are you still sticking your nose where it shouldn't be?"

Marilyn blushed. "It's the Thomas Ballard file."

I had been wishy-washy on this. I had told Marilyn and Steve to review old cases in order to get familiar with how things were done, and I had told them to not look into the Thomas Ballard file. But as time went on, seeing Marilyn doggedly continue to pursue it, I half-heartedly gave her the go ahead to continue. Now I was having second thoughts again, especially when I saw she had listed my father's name in her notebook. I don't necessarily like people snooping into my past. "So find anything new yet?" I asked.

"Well, remember a few months back when we first got hit? I mean when Steve first tore the place apart and all of our files had been tossed about?"

I nodded.

"Well I've been trying to get the files back in order, and interestingly enough, when I was going through Thomas's file, I found an old newspaper clipping that listed the names of the officers at the scene. Then there was something on the news the other day about a disturbance over at that old folk's home, the one out there over at the Presidio Gate, Van Ness."

"I heard something about that," Ozzie injected. "Over by the George Lucas studios."

"Near the old Letterman hospital building," I added. "Heard something about it; a shooting or something."

"Well the shooter at the old folk's home was a former police captain, Brian something. He was involved in the Thomas Ballard case."

"Brian Maloney, from your notes," I added. "Go on."

"Well, he was trying to kill someone, a resident of the old folk's home, an old man. One of the security guards intervened and the gun went off, and…"

"Maloney went off to the wild blue yonder," I quipped. "Any information on who he was trying to get to?"

"I haven't been able to get into the place," Marilyn said. "And there's been nothing more on the news."

"You mean you haven't been able to charm your way into an old folk's home? What kind of detective are you going to be?"

"The front desk lady is a real bitch," Marilyn said. "Says they're currently not accepting any visitors. The second time I went back, she sent out a couple of roughnecks who looked less like orderlies and more like bouncers."

"So what's next?" I asked.

"Aww, Mike. Give me time. Give me time. It's been close to forty years since this case was first closed. Just give me a bit of time. I'll make some progress."

"No doubt," I said, just as Ozzie jumped out of his seat and put up a hand for a high-five.

"We got it!" Ozzie said excitedly.

"Got what?" I asked, happily changing the direction away from my conversation with Marilyn as I slapped Ozzie's hand.

"The location, the company, the address, the phone number, everything!"

"High-five!" Marilyn and I both congratulated Ozzie and his cohorts. "What's its name, where is it located?"

"It's Hoffman International Investments, in the McNamara building down on Market Street."

"Hoffman, that name sounds familiar." I wondered, "Where did I hear it before?"

"Don't know," Ozzie said.

"First time I've heard of it," Marilyn added.

"I know! Got it!" I yelled. "Remember when I told you about the hit man back at Skyline College? Well, intertwined with that whole mess was a little Ponzi land scheme being run out of Half Moon Bay. You remember that, don't you?"

45

"How can we forget!" Marilyn said. "You ended up killing the guy, and I think we all thought you were going away for that one!"

"Self-defense. I plead self-defense," I said. "But you do also remember our searching for a Jessica Windrop, don't you? The assistant of the man who died?"

"Couldn't locate anything about her," Ozzie remembered.

"Except that I found one of her business cards back when I had searched her office, and it had the number for Hoffman International Investments."

"What do they do, what are they known for? Besides hacking into independent businesses?" Marilyn asked.

"It sounded like corporate bullshit when I inquired back then, but why they would be snooping on us, I don't know. Just figuring that out. But also what is strange is that just a couple of days ago, I saw our fabled missing lady, Jessica Windrop."

"What? Where?" Ozzie and Marilyn asked in unison.

"Over in a bar in Pacifica. Our meeting, our brief encounter, or more like my seeing her, was probably just a coincidence, but…"

"So what do you want to know about this company?" Ozzie asked. "I mean, I think I can search around a little. We can always just check their computers directly. Should tell us what you want to know."

"What do you mean?" I leaned forward. "Do you mean…are you saying you can connect to one of their computers and see what they're about?"

"Well, sure. I…" Ozzie smiled. "I mean, my friends and I already had to reverse engineer their little virus. We can connect to their server or computer via the secure tunnels they established and pull whatever we can find on their computers."

"You mean you can hack them back."

"Hack them back," Ozzie confirmed with a huge smile.

"Let's do it. Hack 'em back," I said. "Download anything and everything you can."

"Everything?" Ozzie shook his head. "Doing that will take time and probably more hard drive space than we have here. And if they're on Market Street, they're probably a pretty big company."

"I don't care what it takes," I said. "Fill up these computers and get some external hard drives. Pull in everything you can."

"Everything." Ozzie shook his head.

"Everything. Here." I pulled out our company credit card and handed it to him. "Take Marilyn with you to Best Buy or wherever you need to go, get whatever you need, and start immediately. I'll let Joe know what's going on."

Ozzie's smile grew as he put the card in his breast pocket. "Come on, Marilyn," he said, taking her by the arm. "We have some shopping to do."

That night, I called Joe. I could hear the slots going off in the background. "What casino are you at?"

"None," Joe replied. "We're still at the cabin. Haven't made it out since we got here."

"Oh, I thought I heard slots going off in the background."

"Aw. That's just Marty. He has one of those tablet computers and has some slot games on it. Guess he's itching."

"Well, I've got something to tell you."

"Figured, since you called."

"It's about those break-ins to our offices. I caught the guys."

"Great! Did you give it to them? Are they in custody? Are you OK?"

"Joe," I said. "It was Steve. Steve Parodi."

"Steve?" Joe repeated. "Aw shit. What for? Money?"

"Money for drugs."

"God."

"And there's something else."

"Come on, out with it."

"Sounds like he was coerced to have our offices, our systems, hacked or bugged."

"You sure?"

"I have Ozzie over here right now. He said he found something on our network and all the devices in our offices. He worked out a way to kill it, but right now, I have him doing some reverse hacking; see if we can find out anything about the ones who were running through our stuff."

"Any leads?"

"So far, just a company name, Hoffman International Investments. I think this is tied up with everything that's been happening the last couple of years."

"Could be, could be. I can cut my vacation short, get down there probably in about five hours. Need anything?"

"No, actually, that's all right. Why don't you stay put. I think we're done for the moment. Let's give Ozzie some time. If anything of substance pops up, I'll give you a holler. And you can always try to dig up anything about the Hoffman Company from where you are. I know you have your ways."

Joe laughed. "Yeah, I'll see what I can find, though the Internet up here is the worst, dial-up."

6

For the next couple of days, Ozzie and I kept in constant contact about his hacking and download progress. Most of the data he was pulling in was encrypted, but he said he and his friends had some tools they were using to try to decrypt the data. Marilyn was helping, too. Besides straightening out the office, she was busy taking inventory and categorizing all the data that was being pulled in on an off network computer. Ozzie was filling up hard drives fast and said he would probably have some real information, decrypted and presentable, by the end of the week.

On Thursday afternoon, I received a call from my doctor. The toxicology report had come back, and they had found N-methylphenethylamine in my blood, a hallucinogenic that in combination with the amount of Coumarin found in my blood meant I was partially mickied by a mixture derived from bitter lettuce. Additional chemicals pointed to a natural anesthetic derived from

California poppies, Blue Lotus, skullcap, and several additional as yet unidentified plant species.

Flashback—I remembered Madame Gira, the psychic slash herbalist. She was at the Surf Spot the night I was mickied by the Gorilla, and I remembered she worked somewhere out in Pacifica's Manor district.

I immediately hopped into my car and drove over to the Manor shopping area, parked in front of Colombo's Delicatessen, and began to check the various businesses of the shopping area to see if I could find Madame Gira's place.

She certainly wasn't hard to find. Her shop was on the north side of the shopping area, near the Octopus Lounge. A big purple neon hand with a red flashing neon eye in the palm was in the window of her establishment, though thick black curtains kept prying eyes from seeing deeper inside.

I checked the front door and found it unlocked. When I opened it, a little bell announced that I had entered. I stepped inside, parted a beaded curtain, and found myself in a waiting room where a *Take a Seat* sign hung from a rope interwoven with colorful glass balls. I followed the rules and took a seat in one of the red velvet wing back chairs as I continued to survey my surroundings.

It was pretty astounding that she had been able to transform a rectangular mall box into an otherworldly experience. From the ceiling hung a large fisherman's net filled with colorful glass floaters and starfish that drooped from the edges of the room and was pinned up to the base of a chandelier. The chandelier, made of upturned wine glasses instead of crystals, hung low over a round table with a felt top covered in geometric symbols. A wood folding chair and a throne fit for a king, or in this case, queen, made the table seem off balance.

An ornate bookcase behind the throne was filled with knickknacks that would hinder the removal of any of the dozen leather-bound books that were set behind them. A skull with a dripping candle, a stuffed black cat, and several stuffed ravens were on top of the bookcase as well.

In one corner of the room stood a black electric fireplace that served as what appeared to be a makeshift altar; the mantelpiece of the fireplace contained a variety of seashells filled with smoldering incense, and the smell was nearly stifling. A claw of a crab and the skull of what looked like a mountain lion also shared the space with the acrid incense seashell boats.

Above the fireplace mantelpiece hung a small wooden cross and small paintings of Jesus and Mary of Guadalupe in matching ornate wooden frames. A cuckoo clock loudly ticked, though the sounds were muffled by more heavy dark burgundy curtains, similar to the ones seen from outside, except these were accented with gold fringe and were draped on the walls.

Near the fireplace, and within a step from the round table in the center of the room, was a sideboard that had been painted black, holding a deck of tarot cards, a crystal ball, dice, coins, and what appeared to be the bones of a small animal. To the right of where I sat was another bookcase. This one, however, did not house books, but rather colorful bottles of various shapes and sizes filled with questionable liquids, seeds, and powders of unknown sorts. There was also a pentagram and an astro chart painted in red on what appeared to be goat hides that were attached to a thick black curtain by what looked like bird bones. To my left and above a small table was a naked lamp that contained a blue lightbulb. It bathed the room in a soothing pale light and countered the annoying hum of the neon hand and eye behind the window curtains, and that I was hearing more and more keenly as I sat in my chair looking over the room.

Opposite where I sat, near the front door and by the beaded curtains I had walked through to get into this room, I spotted an abalone shell filled with a sea of crystals and what I guessed were Madame Gira's business cards. It was sitting on another sideboard, and above it was a camera trained on the chairs—and me. As I had been noting my surroundings, I too was being analyzed. Madame Gira would be an expert at picking up any subtle clues of my intentions if I was not careful. Tricks of the trade.

Curtains suddenly parted along the back wall near the fireplace and I was temporarily blinded by bright light emanating from the back room until a figure filled the entrance. When the curtains closed behind the figure and my eyes had readjusted to the darkness of the room, I found Madam Gira standing before me.

Unlike the colorful flannel pajamas and hand-knit purple sweater-vest I had last seen her wearing, she was now in her apparent business attire, a Victorian era long black dress and a black crocheted scarf on her head. As before, her wrists were laden with gold and silver bracelets, but unlike before, she now wore just a single necklace, a silver chain that hung down past her cleavage and contained a thumb-sized quartz crystal.

"I knew you would come," she said in the same deep and sultry voice I remembered hearing back at the Surf Spot.

"And I knew you knew," I smirked. "Especially since I know you know someone you provided with a certain potion, or tincture, last Friday."

"A potion? Last Friday, last Friday, my memory seems to fail me."

"Oh come on, you know. Last Friday, you came up to me, said someone was intent on killing me or something along those lines."

"Oh yes, Mike Mason. I know you. I've been dreaming of you for quite some time. I knew you would come here to visit me, just as I know you are now searching for some answers. You see, I can see your aura, and I can read your energy. I know of your past and present, and I can read your possible future. You are strong, Mike. Yes, you are strong, but you are troubled. Troubled with your life, troubled with what is happening around you. You have come for answers, Mike Mason, and I will guide you. But you, you will have to make your own decisions. You will have to make your own choices. You must choose your own destiny, for I will not tell you what you must do. I will not force you to choose a way; you must decide on your own."

Madame Gira grabbed the stack of tarot cards and took her place on her throne. Putting the stack of cards on the table, with an outstretched hand she offered, "Sit, please."

"Ah no," I said. "Unlike you, I will not give you a choice of what path you will take. I will tell you what path you will take. Firstly, there was a man at the Surf Spot that night we met, and I have a hunch you know him. He is a large Slavic looking fellow, hairy and well dressed. He looks like a gorilla. I believe you either came with him or met with him there. He in turn used whatever you gave him to have me mickied, knocked out. And what I want to know, what I want to know, is what the hell?"

Madame Gira looked at me. Her face was expressionless and it looked as if she was on the verge of faking a trance. "Mike," she said in a husky voice. "Your path, the path you are following, is a path that is not intertwined with my path. Your strands, the links in your story you have put together, do not lead to me, but to others. You must leave and find those you are really in search of."

"Son of a bitch," I cursed. "Do I need to go to the police, have a search warrant made out for this place? Have this placed turned inside out and have the chemicals you have here tested to see if they are allowed in this state—see if any of them match the components of a drug that was found in my system. If traced to something found here, I can have you put you away for a long time."

"Are you through?" Madame Gira calmly asked.

"Not until I get some answers."

"Then sit, please," Madame Gira again offered. "I am open to your inquiries."

I pulled the wooden folding chair closer to the table and sat down. It seemed uncomfortable, rickety, like it would fall to pieces unless I leaned forward onto the table and closer to Madame Gira. I wondered if this was also a trick of her trade.

"First off, I want to know who the man is that you met at the Surf Spot that night."

"I touched many lives that evening, and indeed, Mr. Mason, I believe we both came into each other's circle that evening."

"OK, let me put it this way," I said as I folded my hands on the table. "Were you there on purpose, were you there to meet someone?"

"When you say on purpose, are you asking if I chose to bring myself to that place at that moment? Not all beings have their spirits driven as your spirit guides you, Mr. Mason. My spirit flows and intermingles with the currents of the universe, and I am pulled to places as the divine energies of the universe will have me. I am a floating bottle traveling the ocean currents, and they take me where I need to be at that point and time."

I took a measured breath; this wasn't going to be easy. "Look, let me lay my cards out on the table, so to speak. I too can read people, and you seem like the type of person who likes a calm life around her, one who would rather go about her business and go with the flow, not make any more waves then she needs to. Well, that's not me. That is not the way I roll. Let me warn you, I can make your life complicated, very complicated and uncomfortable, and very quickly."

Madame Gira just looked at me blankly, and I decided it was best to take another route, one where I would be walking on the same street and plane as Madame Gira.

"OK, let me put it this way," I began. "Let's just say that you wake up late some Friday morning, and you have a tea or something, followed by a busy day looking at the sun and smoking some medicinal herbs, when you realize that you are being drawn somewhere, that a current is pulling you, drawing you someplace, you don't know where, just out of here. And you just so happen to grab a bottle or mix up a bottle of something from this display case you have over here, and you find yourself bobbing along like a bottle in the ocean until you come to some land, the Surf Spot way over across town off of Fassler Avenue. And there, as you are bouncing and coming across other beings that have been drawn to this shore, you find this spirit, an unusual one, a big hairy Slavic one, and you feel compelled to give him what you have brought and hidden somewhere on your person. He in turn presses something back into your hand, and then some time later, you see me, and are drawn to me like a moth to a candle and you read from my aura that I am in danger and you must warn me. Is that what happened? Is that what happened, Madame Gira?"

Madame Gira was looking at me as if dumbstruck, her eyes glassy, her mouth moving like she was trying to speak but couldn't. I continued to watch her for a moment, trying to read her lips, trying to determine how much of her was for show or if she was just insane, when I found my hands around the tarot deck. I looked down at the cards and began to finger their worn edges for just a moment, and when I looked back to Madame Gira, she was smiling at me.

I did it. I had broken through to her.

"The man you search for is named Vuk, which in his native tongue means wolf. I have had dealings with him in the past and was there to meet with him and yes, provide him with a tincture. But it was not the one that you must have been given, though I have provided it to him in the past. He comes to me now and again with questions on natural herbs and chemicals, what they do and their purpose. As to what he does with them, that is his karma. I instruct on usage and practicalities, for the difference between any medicine and poison is dosage. For those I come in contact with, those who seek me, for those, I've been nothing more than a vessel of knowledge for those seeking guidance."

"Do you know anything about the persons he was with, another man? I saw him head for another man and a woman, a woman named Jessica Windrop. What can you tell me about them?"

"I know nothing of them. I know only of Vuk, and he is only a distant pupil, one that is blown to these shores when the will of the Divine deems he should return."

Talking to Madame Gira this way was making my head hurt. Or it was the smoldering incense, or maybe it was even the overpowering patchouli oil she had taken a bath in prior to coming out from behind the curtains. In any event, her story seemed plausible enough to me when I translated it into something I could understand—that she had no part in what took place and happened to me that night. She was there just to make a fast buck from a client, a client who shows up now and again asking for some herbal direction.

I pulled out a Coastside Detectives card and tossed it on the table before straightening my jacket. "Next time you hear of Vuk bobbing on these shores, how 'bout giving me a shout out. I feel that his path and mine need to cross again, as willed by the Divine."

I began to stand, and when I did, my bad knee gave out and I nearly fell over, landing on the little table I had been leaning against. When I attempted to stand again, I shook the table and the stack of tarot cards tipped over. One slowly glided, as if by unseen hands, to the floor.

I cleared my throat, straightened up, fixed my coat and tie, kicked my knee out, and made my way toward the beaded curtain.

"Mr. Mason, Mike Mason," Madame Gira called out.

I turned to see her holding the tarot card that had made its way to the floor in her hand. "Days melt into nights, nights back into days, and seasons into years. One day, Mike Mason, this is your fortune."

She turned the card toward me so I could see it; it was that of a man hanging upside down from a tree.

7

FRIDAY MORNING, I RECEIVED a call from Ozzie.

"I am so done! I think I got everything I could and some of the data will probably be duplicative. I filled up all the hard drives on all of our computers plus the external hard drives we bought," Ozzie said. "But more importantly, my buddies and I cracked their encryption and were able to get to everything. Most of it was easy to get into, they were using old 128 byte stuff, but there were some things that took a little more time."

"Ozzie, if I had the money, I'd make you an ivory tower with gold leaf and frescos and fill it with all the women in the world you want!"

"That sounds just as good as dying for virgins in an afterlife." Ozzie laughed.

"So tell me," I asked. "What did you find?"

"I think you need to come on down," Ozzie replied. "I'd rather show you."

The forty-five minute rush-hour drive to the Tenderloin from Pacifica seemed to take hours, but when I got there, I couldn't help but still be in a good mood. Things were moving, and they were going my way. Ozzie had made a breakthrough, and the answers to questions that had been bugging me for the last couple of years were finally falling into place.

When I arrived at the office, I found Ozzie looking ragged and spent. He hadn't slept for a few days and had been running on coffee and power drinks.

"We have massive, just massive, amounts of data. And we still have tons to decrypt, but now that we cracked their security, we can easily open whatever, and whenever we get to it." Ozzie handed me a thumb drive. "Just insert this into any PC, run the application, and it will decrypt their stuff."

"Great." I pocketed the device. "Anything jumping out at you yet?"

"Well, yes," Ozzie said. He pulled out an external hard drive and plugged it into the laptop he was using. "So on a hunch, while we were downloading and after we had broken through their encryption and security, I began to do some random searches on what we had opened, and I came across this."

Ozzie accessed the external hard drive though his laptop and clicked on a folder labeled SP. Inside were tons of documents and zip files. I recognized some of the file names and realized this was some of the data that would have been on our PCs. This was something that had been copied, stolen off our PCs, and Ozzie had just copied it back from one of their PCs or servers. Ozzie then clicked on a pdf marked CSD, and what opened next was a copy of a handwritten note that had a list of names:

Mike Mason
Joe Ballard
Ozzie Ferris
Marilyn Jackson

The listing of names was in Steve Parodi's handwriting. Marilyn's name was heavily underlined.

When my name is on a list, it's rare that I've found it to be a good thing. I was beginning to detest seeing my name in lists. And this was the second time in as many weeks.

"OK," I took a breath. "Next question, do you think they know we have this information?"

"They probably know they've been hacked back," Ozzie pondered, and then added, "Well, maybe not. It all depends on the company; if they are using outside consultants to do their bidding or are doing the work internally, if their IT staff has enough support and understanding to identify a reverse intrusion."

I shook. "This is big. I want you to get everything out of here. Get a storage locker somewhere. All of these computers, hard drives, servers, everything. Let's get it out of here. If they know we have this, they'll come looking sooner rather than later. Call your buddies who helped you, grab Marilyn, and let's clear this place. In fact, let's clear the Marina and Pacifica offices as well. Let me get that hard drive that has all that stuff on it about us. I want to go through it."

Ozzie disconnected the hard drive and passed it to me. "From the specs I got when I downloaded everything, it looks like this data was on a laptop."

"So it's possible we were hacked just from someone who brought in a laptop to a company and not a company itself?"

"Maybe," Ozzie sheepishly agreed.

"God." First I thought we were going to get some company into trouble from hacking us. Now we might be hit for doing it instead. I took another measured breath. "All right, I'll review this hard drive and a couple of these other computers, and you take everything else to storage."

Ozzie got on his phone and began to text his cohorts for help. As he headed out the door, I advised, "When you leave, make sure you aren't followed? Capiche?"

"Yup. Will do," he replied.

WEEK III

8

THROUGHOUT THE WEEKEND, I stayed at our Tenderloin office, only leaving for a short time on Saturday to pick up a couple of shirts from Macy's and stop by the Hilton, where a handshake and a twenty spot placed into an agreeable houseman's hand opened the door to a room where I could take a shower. It wasn't until midnight that night that I came across something that really piqued my interest, an organization chart. The chart was in landscape with five head guys listed, CFOs and the like. At the top of the chart, though, was a Michael Hoffman. You have to hand it to a man who has an international company named after himself. Second from the top right, was a name that jumped out at me, Jasper Hoffman. Was this the same Jasper I was looking for, the one who had scared Max Fortune and in league with the hit man Frank Switch? There couldn't be that many Jaspers around. Sure, there was Jasper's, a bar on O'Farrell and Taylor, and a condominium complex called the Jasper on Rincon Hill near the South of Market area but maybe it was like when you buy a new car, you see that more and more and everywhere.

On Sunday, after attending her father's church, Christ's Light for the Lost, for over three hours, Marilyn joined me in reviewing the contents of the filled and decrypted hard drives. Unsure if we had the time, we printed stacks of documents in various languages, Russian, Chinese, Arabic, and some others that were completely unidentifiable. Ozzie and his buddies, meanwhile, made multiple runs from our different office locations to a storage unit we rented out over on Sixteenth and Bryant, near the San Francisco SPCA. There, they secured all of our office PCs and recently purchased and filled hard drives as a precaution while we worked on comprehending our current situation.

Finally, by Monday morning, all three of our offices has been cleared and it was just me sitting around in our Tenderloin office going through the room full of desks with stacks of paper on them. My back was hurting and my knee was popping. What to do, where to start, and what it all meant was something that was going to take a while, and I was poised to dig in when Marilyn showed up with a couple of cups of coffee.

"Looks like the olden days," I remarked. "Before computers. Now all we just need are some IBM Selectric typewriters."

"Find anything yet?" she asked.

"Not sure," I said. "Aside from the stuff in foreign languages, a lot of it is technical in nature. There appears to be some stuff on mining, a bunch of stuff on ships and underwater retrieval, robots, and the like. There are specs on things that look like engines or vacuums, not sure what it all means. I just don't know."

"Well, then, maybe it's time for a walk," Marilyn suggested. "Loosen things up. You up for it?"

"You know what, maybe that's the way to attack this. Let's go directly to the source, down to Hoffman International Investments, and see if we can talk to the head guy, this…" I picked up the organization chart. "This Michael Hoffman. See what he knows about us being hacked."

Marilyn glanced down to my leg. "You up for that long of a walk?"

"Down to Market Street," I said as I took a sip of my coffee, and Marilyn nodded. "For that long of a walk, let me grab one of my walking sticks from the car. Come on, let's go."

We headed up to the Post Street garage where I had parked the other day when the O'Farrell garage had been full. I retrieved a couple of rolls of quarters and pondered which of the canes to take. Eventually, I decided upon the Zap Cane that was in my car's trunk.

"That looks brutal," Marilyn commented.

"From Joe," I replied.

"Figures."

From the garage, we headed down Post to Powell Street, walking along the Saint Francis Hotel side of the street, across from Union Square. As we crossed Geary and continued down Powell, streetcar bells clanging away as we dodged tourists from all over the world, I couldn't help but be struck by the changes in this part of the city since I had last been there. Gone were the little shops I grew up with, the camera and luggage shops that had been run for decades by olive-skinned Middle Eastern men with collared shirts and thick mustaches, banners noting they were in the middle of a going out of business sale, with everything at huge discounts. They'd been going out of business for decades, and were constantly at odds with the city.

Bars that I used to frequent, too, such as the bawdy and gaudy Gold Dust Lounge, with its theater-style marquee, once patronized by both famous and infamous San Franciscans as well as those visiting from Los Angeles and Hollywood were gone. Gone too were their near fabled employees, such as the old man who stood out front of the Gold Dust wearing a fedora and a yellow plaid wool suit, checking IDs before you were allowed into the room adorned with velvet tapestries and photos of naked women. With that bouncer being reminiscent of a Columbus Street barker, you weren't sure if you were entering a bar, a strip club, or a brothel. And the drinks were always strong and cheap.

All these places from my memories had been replaced by corporations; Walgreens drug store, H&M and Express clothiers, Swarovski, Sketchers, and the like. The sidewalks that had been widened and cleaned were now routinely patrolled by police. The city had successfully transformed a once gritty and vibrant small business marketplace into a clean vanilla corporate dominated shopping district via redevelopment dollars.

When we reached the end of Powell at Market Street, just beyond the cable car turnaround and the line of tourists snaking a path from one side of Powell to the other, Marilyn and I paused so I could shake out my knee.

Back in the day when Joe and I worked this side of town, I used to know the names of all the classic old downtown buildings and high rises, as did Joe. But it had been a while, and it took me a few moments to recall the name of the big old stone serpentine colored building we were standing in front of.

I snapped my fingers. "The Flood Building."

"Yes. Yes it is," Marilyn commented. "Remember back in the day this street level used to be Woolworths, and you could go downstairs where they had a pet department?"

"And the lunch counter and a candy bar, where you could get hot toasted cashews," I replied.

"Ah-ha," Marilyn agreed. "And across the street was the Emporium, and at Christmas, there would be Santa and an ice skating rink."

I glanced across Market Street. The Emporium had been replaced decades ago by the Westfield San Francisco Center and Bloomingdales.

"I remember when cable car conductors would ask for help spinning the cars around so they could head back up Powell Street hill."

"That was before the refurbishment of the system, back in the eighties."

"Yup."

I turned my attention back to the dark green edifice called the Flood Building. The bottom floor was no longer a Woolworths. The space was now taken up by the Gap clothing store. Large colorful banners filled the upper windows, the contrast of the bright colors to the green patina of the building looked like a desecration to me, and I commented as such as we began our walk down Market.

"I don't know," Marilyn said. "Maybe it's the artist in me, but I like it. It kind of reminds me of a stained glass window. The bright colors of glass framed by copper framing."

"Ha! Too bright," I replied as we began walking down Market.

Market is a street of wonders, a time capsule of a stretch of San Francisco history running east to west that can be broken down into three sections.

From the Embarcadero and the Ferry Building at the foot of the Bay to Powell, lower Market is old San Francisco, a high-rise grandeur of the early twentieth century. Any number of buildings intrigue the eye, many of which have lobbies containing documentation of their storied history, such as the Flood Building, where there is a replica of a famous black bird that at one time resulted in the deaths of several San Franciscans. This stretch of pavement also contains many statues and artifacts of a bygone era; a blue and gold leafed clock, Lotta's fountain, the statue of a multitude of naked men working an oversized press.

The north side of lower Market, the Financial District, contains buildings from the sixties through late nineteen seventies, while the south side was currently in the process of being redeveloped into a housing metropolis hub of the uber wealthy, a recent phenomena for San Francisco that began with the Mission Bay development, a wholesale replacement of square miles of small manufacturing, vacant land and affordable housing with high-tech genetic research, manufacturing and high-rise condominiums for the overpaid.

Mid-Market, the area roughly from Powell to Octavia, has so far been able to maintain a seedy grittiness that has successfully fended off the surrounding developments. The city has tried to get a foothold in the area, offering some high-tech firms such as Twitter free rent and tax incentives to set up shop, but with the area bordering the Tenderloin district and equally degraded Sixth Street neighborhood, or Hood, the city will have a long way to go.

Upper Market, roughly from Octavia to Castro, is home to many small businesses interwoven with large companies that have crammed themselves into small window shops. This area, especially at Market and Castro, is defined as the home of the ever-expanding acronym LGBTQIA and community. Rainbow colored banners hang from the streetlights and rainbow flags adorn both homes and businesses. Buildings to the north of upper Market tend to be old apartment buildings, while to the south, small apartment and single family homes dominate the landscape.

When we left Powell, we continued east down lower Market toward the Ferry Building, passing the wedged-shaped Phelan Building and the copper-domed Hobart Building, both survivors of the 1906 earthquake and fire.

This part of Market Street really has maintained its grandeur, even with the sprinkling of modern skyscrapers. The historic trolleys from all over the world that run up and down Market add to the time capsule feel of the area. At street intersections, though, looking toward this section of South of Market, you see evidence of the current economic boom affecting the area. Buildings taller than the iconic Pyramid Building in the Financial District going up at a record pace and number, clusters of them, destined to be marvels of engineering and probably stupidity when a large earthquake finally hits.

As we continued, I realized I was really enjoying our walk down Market, reminiscing about earlier times, when Marilyn and I were both kids and didn't have a care in the world. And I was beginning to really enjoy being around Marilyn. There's a lot to be said about having common experiences with someone your own age. That is, until she decided to bring something back up.

At New Montgomery, I convinced Marilyn to join me for a drink at The Palace Hotel, San Francisco's oldest surviving hotel, and although she's a teetotaler, I said I needed to stop because my knee was beginning to bug me. She acquiesced, and once inside, thanked me profusely for convincing her to take the break.

"Lots of history here," I said as I proudly escorted her around the garden court, a lavish stained glass three-story domed banquet hall with crystal chandeliers.

"This too burned to its shell during the 1906 earthquake and fire."

I had to smile as Marilyn oohed and aahed while we strolled the courtyard, heading for the hotel bar.

"President Harding died here, but rumor has it something happened to him over at the House of Shields, an old bar across the street. It was during Prohibition, and he drank too much or something, was already sick, fighting pneumonia, and was taken through a tunnel from the House of Shields bar to his hotel room where he eventually died."

We found seats at the Pied Piper Bar, rich wood paneling mosaic tile floor, paintings, and old photographs throughout. Above the bar hangs a massive painting, *The Pied Piper of Hamelin* by Maxfield Parrish.

I ordered a Manhattan and for Marilyn, a Shirley Temple.

"So I've found something interesting in regard to the Thomas Ballard file," Marilyn said as she sipped her ginger ale drink.

"Yes?"

"Remember the other day on the news about Brian Maloney trying to kill someone at the old folk's home?"

I nodded.

"Well, it sounds like he was actually trying to kill someone in that place, and the person he was trying to kill was someone by the name of Roosevelt Jones."

"The same Roosevelt Jones who was the sole witness to Thomas Ballard's murder and who went missing back in the seventies?" I was in shock. I took a big swig of my drink, snapped and pointed to my half-filled glass to get the bartender's attention for a refill, and motioned to Marilyn to continue.

"Probably, I mean, how many people out there do you think are named Roosevelt Jones?"

"Well did you get hold of him, talk to him, ask him what was going on, now and back then?"

"I've been trying to get a hold of him," Marilyn said, then shook her head in disappointment. "But so far, no luck. I still can't get past the nag at the front door of the place. I can't even get through the front patio anymore without one of her goons coming through the front door after me."

"Roosevelt Jones," I mused. "If I remember right, he was initially interviewed, but really didn't say much. He then disappeared."

"Skipped town is more like it, out of fear. Turns out he had moved to New Orleans. Took his son, Lyndon, with him."

"Really, Lyndon?" I said incredulously.

Marilyn smiled. "Yup. Lyndon. Anyway, after hurricane Katrina, Lyndon came to San Francisco. He moved into the Tenderloin, and well, he's been working here as a fry cook at a couple of places ever since. He even does a shift at Sloppy's."

"Damn, small world." I shook my head. "And how did you find all of this out? Get in contact with him?"

"Through my dad's church. I had my dad ask around if anyone knew a Roosevelt Jones, and sure enough, Lyndon was in the audience. We hooked up and I asked Lyndon why Brian Maloney, the ex-police captain, had tried to kill his father. He said his father didn't know. Never met him. Didn't know why anyone would want to kill him. That he was just an old man trying to live the rest of his life."

"Did you ask Lyndon if he knew anything about the Thomas Ballard murder?"

"Yes, I asked him. And he said he knew nothing about it. Said he would ask his father about it."

"Hmm." I emptied my first glass and started my second as Marilyn took a courtesy sip of hers.

"Mike," Marilyn said as she put a hand on my wrist and tried to look into my eyes. "Can I ask you something personal?"

Her hand on my wrist naturally caught my attention, but when she asked if she could ask me something personal, I kinda knew what was coming next. I looked to the painting, *the Pied Piper of Hamlin*, and tried to dissect the image.

"Sure," I replied after taking a mouthful of my Manhattan.

"Mike," Marilyn continued, unfazed by my reaction to her question. "I know this might be a little too personal for you, but what can you tell me about your childhood? About your father? I mean, is he even still alive?"

"What can I tell you about my father." I pondered the question, for it wasn't something I was comfortable discussing.

"Well," I finally said. "I can tell you I haven't seen him in decades, lost track of him when my mother disappeared, and I was kicked out onto the streets. I can tell you he was a cop, an old-school cop, the type of cop you found all over the country in the seventies, the type who would bend or skirt the law to fit his needs. Hard, tough, stern, racist, and generally an asshole. It was either his way or no way, so we butted heads a bunch as I was growing up. He was abusive. I remember the fights he would get in with my mom. One-sided fights normally, with him slapping her around as they both were screaming. I remember the last one especially clearly, the last one they had just before she left. It was in the kitchen. They had been fighting about something and he was choking her, and at the moment, I really thought he was going to kill her. And she was managing to egg him on by saying, 'Do it, do it!' I came in and tried to pull one of his hands away, and he pushed me away, so I came back and started to karate chop at his arm and he pushed me away again. But I guess he came to his senses, because he released his grip and walked out of the house."

I could feel the memory choking me up and I motioned to the bartender for a refill, my third.

"So he was that kind of guy," I said.

"And your mother never tried to contact you?"

"Nope. Never heard from her again. No note, no nothing. My dad said she had run off with someone from the neighborhood and good riddance."

74

I swirled the three cherries on their stick in my new Manhattan. "Shortly after that fight, my mom left us, and not too long after that, I was kicked out of the house. By that time, I was already doing some work for Joe at the first Coastside Detectives office in the Tenderloin, the one at the old location. I used to see my father now and again down there, and at first he tried to make contact with me, just to yell or be an asshole. He actually brought me into the station on some trumped up charges now and again. Just being an asshole. Then I started to fight back, get lawyers, and actually was able to get a restraining order on him. After that, he just ignored me if we crossed paths. If there was an issue where police were involved and he was around, he would just melt back into the scene and out of sight. Sometime in the eighties, I just stopped seeing him. Not sure if he moved to another district or department, was fired, retired, or died. I just don't know. And in all actuality, I really don't care."

As I was talking, Marilyn listened intently, now and again taking a sip of the Shirley Temple she had been nursing as I had gulped down my drinks. I was now feeling a little shaky. I think it was more from me revealing my personal life than from the alcohol, but in any event, I was no longer feeling comfortable in my seat.

"Come on," I said, grabbing my cane. "Let's head out."

Marilyn slung her purse over her shoulder, grabbed my arm, and smiled. "You OK?"

"Yes," I said as I stood and kicked out my bad leg. "Just stiffening up. Come on, let's go," I said, attempting to rush us out of the space.

As we left The Palace Hotel, I had to assure myself of two things. "Marilyn," I said. "What I just told you, that is just between us. And don't mention anything to Joe about the headway you've now made in this case. I don't want him to get worked up. Not until we have all the facts."

Marilyn responded by hitting me across the chest with her purse. "Who do you think I am, talking about people, about their personal lives behind their backs? And I already know not to talk to Joe."

That was what she said, but I suspected she already had been talking to him, trying to get as much info as she could about the Thomas Ballard case, as she was doing with me.

We continued down Market, the Ferry Building growing larger and larger as we came closer to the end of Market, until we reached Freemont Street, where we stepped off of Market and headed toward Mission. Immediately, you could see the change in the direction the city was headed. Tall glass skyscrapers filled the sky. Massive projects, one right next to the other, the density so high, you could only see a sliver of the sky directly above you.

At the corner of Freemont and Mission stands one of the newer all black glass buildings in the area, the McNamara. Our destination.

Named in honor of a former San Francisco police chief, and the only thing classy about the building, the McNamara looked as if it was designed to impose its will on this South of Market neighborhood and the other buildings in the area. Along the sidewalk and surrounding the building were square pyramid shaped reinforced concrete barriers that replaced the line of trees normally installed along sidewalks in the city's march to create an urban forest. These Dragon's Teeth, as they were commonly known during World War II, complement the supposed to be art installation of a giant set of jacks, a big cement ball and individual steel girder installations that are reminiscent of hedgehog tank traps. With video cameras perched in every direction at the entrance of the building, and a white shirted security guard at the front entrance, the overall feeling and architectural style of the building is that of Modern Intimidation.

As I studied the building from where we stood kitty-corner at a stoplight, I found Marilyn was preoccupied with something else.

"Wow!" she said. "Over there. We got time for me to check that out?"

I looked to where Marilyn's attention had been drawn, and in the pull through of the building directly across from the McNamara was an overly developed recreational vehicle, pullouts fully extended. The entire vehicle was painted in bright colors with pictures of clothes and the words WOW Wardrobes on Wheels.

"Sure," I said. "No rush."

We crossed the street and Marilyn climbed inside the mobile retail establishment. I could hear the cackle of women's laughter inside and their commenting on how things looked on each other. When Marilyn came out, she was all smiles, but as we crossed the street to the McNamara, she commented, "I've been wanting to see one of those after I heard about them on the news and about them running around downtown like the food trucks. Nothing that I would buy though. Looks like they just raided Ross a couple of years ago and upped the price."

The first level guard, the doorman of the McNamara, asked to see our badges to enter, and when we replied we were there for a meeting, he just opened the door and allowed us in.

"The next one won't be so easy," I whispered to Marilyn as we headed for the next guard, sitting in a commanding position in a bunker shaped module next to a metal detector.

We paused before we reached the guard and glanced at the occupancy board.

"Looks like the building is mostly empty. Nothing until about a dozen floors below the Hoffman suite, and nothing above it."

"Can I help you?" the guard asked from behind his station, his voice echoing in the otherwise open and vacant lobby.

"I'm here to see Mister Hoffman" I said. "Michael Hoffman."

"Is he expecting you?"

"He should be."

"And you are?"

I pulled out my card and handed it to the guard. He read it, gave me a sideways look, and then picked up his phone. "I have a Mister Mike Mason from Coastside Detectives to see Mister Michael Hoffman."

There was a pause as he listened to what was being said by the party on the other end of the line. "No," he finally said. "He has someone with him. A woman. Short. Black. Heavy set."

"Oh no you didn't," Marilyn said.

The guard looked disgusted at Marilyn as he hung up the phone and said, "You," as he held my card out between two fingers to pass it back to me. "You can go. But you," he said, talking to Marilyn, "can sit over there." He pointed to a brown patent leather bench against the wall.

I started to walk toward the metal detector. "And that," he said pointing to the Zap Cane, "Stays here. With her. Or with me. In any event, it is not going beyond here. Do you need a wheelchair or something?"

I just smiled, nodded, and handed Marilyn the cane as I began the normal dress down before passing through the metal detector.

"Twenty-second floor, when you get off the elevator, you will see a pair of double doors facing you," the guard said. "Go through those, and a secretary will help you. You will be seeing Jasper Hoffman, Michael Hoffman is not in."

When the elevator doors opened on the twenty-second floor, I found two gentlemen waiting for me. One was the same guy who had slipped me a mickey back at the Surf Spot, the guy with the extraordinarily hairy chest and flat nose, Vuk, the Gorilla. He smiled when he saw me.

"How'd you like your Pisco sour?" he asked as he maintained his stupid grin.

"Peachy," I said. "Just peachy."

"Nice kick, Don't you think?"

"Not bad," I replied. "But the next round is on me."

The Gorilla's sidekick looked as if he had been getting too much sun; his face was covered with freckles and moles. I decided his name would be Moleman and as I stepped out of the elevator, the Gorilla pushed me up against a wall as Moleman frisked me. When he came to my coat pockets, he found the rolls of quarters and handed them to the Gorilla. I sarcastically asked, "You going to feed the meter for me?"

He just grunted and dropped the rolls back into my coat pocket and pulled me off the wall. "Come on, funny man."

As they escorted me arm in arm, I had a better view of Moleman's face. Some of the darker moles looked asymmetrical. "You should get those looked at," I said. "Could be cancerous."

"Funny man!" the Gorilla repeated. Moleman yanked on my arm, indicating I should pipe down and continue moving.

"Just looking out for your well-being," I said as we came to a pair of double doors flanked by frosted safety glass. Through the glass, I could just about make out the figure of a woman behind a desk. A buzzer went off, the doors were unlocked, and we entered.

Inside, I found myself peering at a tall buxom Asian woman who had stood up to greet us. Behind her was a desk and another set of double doors bookcased with more thick chicken-wired safety glass. Through the glass I could see there was a line of offices along what appeared to be an I-shaped floorplan. Facing her, and behind me were dual banks of monitors that filled the walls, telling me on a quick glance that she kept a watchful eye on all hallways and some rooms. One monitor was showing something different, though, some sort of underwater documentary. It appeared several small submersible robots were coasting along the ocean floor.

"Good morning." The woman smiled and came out from behind her desk to stand before me with an outstretched hand.

I shook my escorts off my arms, straightened my tie, fixed my hair, and with the warmest of smiles, shook her hand and replied, "Good morning to you, too!"

"You're expected," she said as she turned to unlock the second set of doors. I watched her as she moved, as did my companions, but her next orders frosted the warm feeling she initially gave me. "Take him to the Gallery."

As we passed through this second set of double doors and paused, I looked quickly to my left and right to get the lay of the land. Both sides ended relatively quickly at a blank wall, and both had closed solid doors bearing signs that were small enough and at an angle to where I was standing so that I could not read them. Straight ahead in front of me, a parallel line of offices went down a long hall, at the end of which was a large floor to ceiling window with a panoramic view that looked out upon Fremont and Market Streets.

As I was taking in the layout of the office and feigning my inspection with a "Wow, look at that view" for my escorts' benefit, I was suddenly struck by the appearance of a familiar feminine profile silhouetted with the backdrop of the city as she made her way across the far end of the hallway.

"Jessica!" I yelled.

Jessica Windrop was startled, naturally, but she carried herself well, pausing only momentarily to look toward me before continuing on her way and out of my line of sight.

"She's a looker," I said and the response I got from the Gorilla was a knock on my shoulder with his shoulder. We continued down the hall and as we walked down the aisle of offices, I could see that each office had a flat-screen television set attached to the wall showing the same underwater science show as in the reception area. Behind each glass wall and office door facing the corridor, there were people busy working on one thing or another, though I couldn't take in much of what they were doing, as the Gorilla and Moleman were keeping up the pace.

At the end of the hall, we made a left and walked along a hallway, the full-length windows on my right had views of San Francisco up to Twin Peaks. At the end of this hall was a set of double doors. A sign on one of the doors read the Gallery. Moleman opened the door and motioned with an arm for me to enter.

"Not joining me?" I asked, and the Gorilla pushed me inside. They shut and locked the doors behind me.

9

THE GALLERY WAS SITUATED on the southeast corner of the McNamara and standing there, looking straight ahead, the room's glass walls offered me views of the Bay Bridge, the East Bay hills, and everything as far south as the eye could see. A large dark wood meeting table stretched and filled the center of the room, surrounded by chairs. The wall to my left was solid and contained a trio of macabre and abstract paintings framed in gaudy gold leaf. The wall at the far end of the room had a single door and a gigantic mirror framed with dark wood and bookended by speakers. Above the mirror was a large flat-screen television that flickered on as I approached. Again, the same underwater documentary appeared, silent moving submersible robots scouring the sea floor.

I walked over to the mirror, fixed my hair and tie, and put my finger up to the mirror. I could see it was a two-way mirror, just like Rochelle, Rich Fortune, had mentioned to me many years ago, and just as I expected.

I waved to the people I knew were on the other side of the mirror, then found a chair where I could sit and wait.

The wait wasn't long. A man's voice came from the speakers on either side of the mirror, and I could hear in the background what I surmised was the talk of the submersible divers: that tinny crackling sound of radio communications from sea to ship, or in this case, possibly from ship to shore.

"Mr. Mason, I've been expecting you, although I didn't expect you to take so long to figure out where to find me. And my, my, my…you've come to pay us a visit on a red letter day." The man then chuckled and continued. "Or may I call you Mike? Mister Mason sounds so formal and seems odd for me to say aloud."

"Sure." I shrugged. "And may I take it you are Jasper Hoffman?"

"Yes, you are correct."

"And how do you wish to be addressed? As Jasper, or as *The Hoff*?"

The man let out a slight chuckle. "Jasper is fine, and now that we have the formalities out of the way, how may I help you?"

"Well, you can start by telling me why you have shown such interest in me and why you've been hacking into our computers."

"Now Mike, what would bring you to such a conclusion?"

"We found your little bug. The one you had installed on one of our computers to spy on us. We reverse engineered that little guy and it led us back to your company, and in particular, to a laptop that contained a pdf marked CSD."

"What? I…when?"

I heard some whispering in the background. Apparently, no one had mentioned to his highness that we had worked our way back into his tower.

"Very well. So you discovered that we've been listening and watching you from afar." He then laughed. "You are turning out to be everything I had hoped for, so yes, you are under my eye, ever since your run-in with Laura Grandviewer. Well actually, that isn't quite true. I've known of you long before that, longer than you could ever realize."

His voice changed as he barked out a command. "Jessica," he said. "It is time you left us. Please, through the Gallery."

From where I was sitting, I watched as the door handle that led to the room behind the mirror turned. The door clicked open and out walked Jessica Windrop.

"Long time no see," I said.

"So nice to see you again, Mister Mason."

"I see you haven't upgraded your choice of company," I said to Jessica.

"Oh, I have Mr. Mason. I have."

"I take it you two have met before," Jasper interrupted.

"Oh, yes." I replied, "We have a mutual acquaintance, a Mister Darrell Harsher, her former employer. I take it you know him quite well too, as you sent a hit man through him to try to take me out."

"Jessica!" Jasper's voice nearly broke over the speakers before he regained his composure. "Please, continue on your way."

I watched as Jessica sauntered out of the room. "That's one thing I have to give you," I said as she made her way out of our view. "You certainly make good choices in picking your employees."

"Ah, yes, I'm glad you approve." Jasper sounded content.

"Now let's get back to why you sent a hit man after me, that Frank Switch. I don't take kindly to those who come after me, or those who sent them. Why did you send him after me, anyway?"

"Come, come now, Mike. Don't get into such a tizzy. And you know why he was sent after you. You killed Rich Fortune, Max's Fortune's wife. So yes, I did authorize the release of Mr. Frank Switch, a mediocre hit man to say the least, to Max Fortune to do his bidding. However, you must admit, Max did have a legitimate beef with you and if you must know, it was truly out of my hands at that point."

I could hear Jasper take an annoyed and measured breath over the speaker. It was fine with me that I was annoying him with my questions. I wanted the answers.

"Max had done so much for Hoffman International Investments," Jasper continued, "and was instrumental in many of our various endeavors. His commitment and loyalty literally tied my hands when he approached and requested—well, demanded—revenge. Some of our silent investors, our associates, expected something to be done as well, once you had, shall I say, silenced, his wife, Rochelle Fortune. Releasing Frank Switch to Max became partly professional courtesy and partly obligation. Max's attempt on your life through Frank Switch was for his revenge, not mine. I must say, I will not block a man bent on revenge when he has good cause. And in any event, you and your partner...Joe Ballard, isn't it?"

"Yes."

"You two did succeed in defending yourselves, as I thought you would, by killing Frank in that parking lot."

"And you killed Max Fortune in the hospital. Just so he couldn't spill the beans about you."

"Ah, Max," Jasper agreed, "at that point, was expendable. Or more succinctly, a liability. But no, I did not kill him. Someone more adept and in Frank Switch's line of work did what needed to be done."

"Was that person Vuk?" I asked, knowing Vuk, the Gorilla's propensity for using drugs to take people out. Max had fallen into the big sleep after someone had poisoned him with Saxiton while he was recuperating in the hospital.

"My, my, my, you have done your homework. But no, I know nothing of Max's death, just that it was probably best for him to leave at that time."

I stared deeply into the two-way mirror and contemplated what Jasper had just told me.

He interrupted my thoughts. "Mike, if I wanted you dead, you would be dead. Many opportunities have been made available. That incident at the restaurant, although Vuk got a little carried away, was just one of many instances where you could have been silenced. It is not what I want done. And if I did want to take you out, I would have done it more discreetly, and in private. I would keep it tidy and make sure you were comfortable."

"I'll give that to you; you have a way of tiding things up, like with the silencing of Max Fortune, even though you won't admit it. And I'm pleased to hear that you wish to make things comfortable for me, though I'm not pleased to hear about the circumstances in which you wish to make me comfortable."

"I'm glad you approve of our methods of business. And with that, it brings us to your original question when you first arrived in my offices. Why I've had such a strong interest in you."

"You can say that again."

"Walk over to the windows."

I looked toward the panoramic windows from my seat. "Yes, get up," Jasper insisted. "Go over there and tell me what you see."

I climbed out of my chair, my knee popping, but I continued walking without interruption until I reached the windows and could peer out onto Bay Bridge, the East Bay Hills and on the South of Market and Rincon Hill areas of the city. "I see the East Bay, and in the city, I see buildings. Lots of new buildings going up everywhere." It was actually quite impressive, seeing a city grow out of a neighborhood.

Tons of new buildings going up. Cylinders of glass, rectangular blocks, and crystal spires. It looked like an architect's vision of Bryce Canyon.

"Beautiful, isn't it?" Jasper asked. Not waiting for my answer, he continued, "Almost an impenetrable wall of glass, wouldn't you say? Inspiring. Emblematic of wealth and power and, hmmm, I am proud to say I've had a hand in making all of what you see before you."

I walked the length of the window. It was amazing. This part of the city was now unrecognizable as what I had known of the area growing up. Gone were most of the two to four story buildings and factories of the turn of the century. Those few left had large *For Sale* signs on them and would soon be replaced by an empty lot, a hole, and then a new high-rise.

"The city wanted this area to be revitalized, and they've gotten it, in spades, wouldn't you say?"

I could just about picture Jasper smiling like the Cheshire Cat.

"Cheap land and interest rates at all-time lows allowed my company to buy up everything you see here and collaborate with other companies to build this, this city within a city, a city that you see rising before you."

"Acquired and developed legally, I take it."

"And acquired and developed all legally. At least I can attest to that on my part. Well, mostly."

"Is that why there's a giant new condominium complex right over there," I said pointing toward Rincon Hill as if he was standing beside me, "named the Jasper?"

"Surely you don't think I have that big of an ego to name a building after myself."

At this point, I could almost hear Jasper smirk as I continued to gaze at the myriad of buildings that were in various stages of completion. I counted over twenty-five new high rises and lost count on the number of cranes.

"It is awe inspiring, wouldn't you say," Jasper continued. "And at this stage, it is almost all residences. Each unit going for many millions of dollars, and with the new laws enacted and embraced by the city, most are just double the size of a jail cell. Isn't that something? We can cram more people in and get more money per square foot than we could ever get selling space to a business."

"It is amazing," I agreed. "I just wonder, though. You have people, say, in this building, who bought their condo for the view, and now a new building comes up and their bay view has been replaced by a view of the building right next to them. Reminds me of a time when builders just did that sort of thing out of spite. And all of this building, all of these high rises packed in so close together, it makes me wonder what happened to the original fears people use to bandy about the Manhattanization of San Francisco."

"Ha!" Jasper laughed. "I remembered those worries and cries as well. The Manhattanization of San Francisco! Pshht. I'm the one who set the groundwork for what is happening here and now, right in front of everyone's eyes, and most don't even realize it. They can't comprehend what they are seeing. It is only if you go to one of the buildings on the edge of this new frontier, like this one, the McNamara, or as you view the area from the Bay Bridge or drive through the area that you realize what is happening. And this is just the beginning. There will be more. Land in San Francisco is a cash cow. You just have to get those in power to agree with you, and those who do not, or could say or have the sway to do something, can have their thoughts on the idea changed with oh so little cash. That worry of the San Francisco skyline changing to resemble Manhattan, that was played out, or rather, paid out, to those who had a say a long time ago."

"Humph." I found it a bit distressing to hear and to see this change in my city right in front of me, without me hardly noticing it, as well.

And to see all the history disappear in such a ruthless and casual fashion. There had to be something that could be done to slow things down.

So I had to ask. "Wasn't there something called the Shadow Ordinance, or something along that line? Some ordinance that the city or neighbors could use to limit the heights of buildings? I remember something about if a building would cast a shadow for too many hours per day on a local city park, it could not be built."

"That one makes me laugh, too." And Jasper did. "What you see before you was a place that was mostly industrial. An area of mixed use, vacant lots, abandoned buildings, old factories, and railroad right-of-ways. This was the remaining industrial heart of the city, so there were no parks here for us, for my development to cast shadows on. But true, that concern was raised. That ordinance has been invoked, even recently, in some of the smaller neighborhoods to halt construction that will eventually come. And yes, in those cases, the construction of buildings even four stories tall were thwarted. But here, just look over to the new Transbay Transit Center and Towers being built on the site of the old Transbay bus terminal on Second Street or the Salesforce building. When those buildings are complete, they will be the tallest buildings on the West Coast, the shadow of which can touch basically most of the city at some point in the day. Indeed, shadows of most of our buildings cross over to the surrounding neighborhoods, casting them into darkness during daylight, but as with most things now days, cash and a little technology can sway those who are willing to be swayed. For each development, we showed through a computer program how much of a shadow the building would cast, for how long, and the percentage of the decrease in sunlight reaching an area on a typical sunny day. A building taken individually in this area can, for the most part, have minimal impact. And by the ordinance, you are taking just this one building into account. The ordinance does not consider the shadow impact of a group of buildings on an area. So yes, when all of this construction is complete, we can cast a wall of shadows over a good portion of the city, for a good portion of the day, even with local laws against such."

I pressed my head against the window and looked directly down toward the street far below. The further down I looked, the darker it appeared to be, sort of like looking down a rectangular well. "It would be nice for the people out on the street to get some sunshine. There's something to be said about quality of life, not just in the material objects. Buildings and money. For a city known for fog, just a little bit of sunshine for the ordinary folks down below is sometimes nice. For the little people. The ordinary folks living and working down there who can't afford to live in buildings like these."

"You're beginning to sound a bit like those Occupy Wall Street protestors who for a time made some noise out there. The so-called Ninety-Nine Percenters. Do you see them now? Do you hear of them now? This is the new San Francisco. The people who live, really live, not just survive, in San Francisco, are either ones with money or are holding onto what they can. The ones who are just holding on are being replaced by those with the money, and soon there will be just two, those with, and those without. The others, or ones who live on the streets, scraping out a living by holding down three jobs, why should I worry about them? The left-leaning Occupy Wall Street protestors that are made up of them and cried that it was time for the tide to change for the poor. They were almost immediately countered by the political Tea Party movement, who said they were here to stem the changing tide toward socialism, and bring back good ol' American capitalism. Remember that? Both claimed to be part of the Ninety-Nine Percenters. But there's little difference between the Occupy Wall

Street protestors and the Tea Party movement. Both wish to bring down the US economy, reshuffle the deck, as two sides of the same coin, with the Tea Party being a bit more successful than the latter, shutting down the government for a time, shaking the world's economy to the point where the IMF, the International Monetary Fund, agreed to a long-term plan to replace the US dollar with the Chinese Yen as the world's currency."

"Two sides of the same coin," I repeated.

"Exactly," Jasper said. "And you know what, I'm glad to let them wear that badge, the Ninety-Nine Percenters. While they are down there fighting among themselves, I get to look down and laugh."

"You know what?" I said, turning from the view and walking to the two-way mirror. "You're just like what I've pictured as the One Percenters. What both groups have portrayed as the One Percenters… an uncaring, uncompromising, corrupt businessman who just thinks about himself and is only interested in acquiring more wealth and power."

"And what's wrong with being that, a successful businessman? No, no, no, no, no. Just because I've risen above most of the people in this world by getting out of my seat to grasp the brass ring, that doesn't make me a villain, does it? And that is what you are calling me, a villain, aren't you? No, you shouldn't call someone that just because they are successful in life. No, those who should be called villains are those who will take advantage of a situation, such as…hmm…let's just say, hypothetically mind you, if through their bickering and fighting, both groups, Occupy Wall Street and the Tea Party movement, eventually became my foot soldiers to take someone, well like me, to where I want to be."

"And where's that?"

"What if I was to tell you I am on the verge of becoming one of the most powerful men in the world? Would you believe me? And I will eventually use both groups, along with some others, to bring me there."

"Possibly," I said. "Just one thing. You missed the boat. That Occupy Wall Street movement is gone." I laughed. "No funding."

"But the sentiment is there. As you said, they are down there, scratching out a living," Jasper countered. "They are just sleeping soldiers. They will rise up and do as I bid, as will the Tea Party and other groups as I orchestrate future social and political events around the world." He laughed. Laughed like a lunatic as I went back to my chair and sat down.

"All right, Doctor Strangeglove," I said. "So I take it you are planning to do something that isn't quite legal, similar to some of your other ventures. From what I can tell, your seed money originally came via your black market dealings with Laura Grandviewer and possibly your property flipping ventures with Jessica's former employer, Darrell Harsher. My only question is," I asked as I leaned forward in my chair and whispered, "does your new venture with the Occupy Wall Street and Tea Party movement in any way involve this underwater show you have playing on all of your TVs? You had said earlier it was a red letter day."

I could just about hear Jasper smirking again. "Yes. Yes, you can say that. You can say this underwater show is just the first step, even the step before the prelude. It is the orchestra getting into their seats and warming up. And no. All of those little ventures before, those with Laura Grandviewer, and all of those little, minor offenses; those were all trivial, tri-vi-al endeavors. I had already made my money, raised enough capital to begin my monopoly of the area you see beyond that window. No, what you came across, and what I let you see, those were the last of my remaining outliers. Just little dangling strings of a big ball that I used to go fishing. Fishing for you. To test you. To see what you were made of."

"What?"

"Mike, I've been following you for a while now. And I've come to know you quite well."

"Well, yeah, by spying on us through our computers."

Jasper just tossed my comment away. "Your sense of humor—I find it less and less amusing, especially now that I am beginning to know of your true leanings. Since we were just talking about it, who do you align yourself with, Mike? Since you are not at my level, a One Percenter, a businessman, or a villain, if you wish, who do you see yourself as being? An Occupy Wall Street type of person, or a Tea Party type of person?"

"Neither," I said flatly. "And since you said you were planning on using both for some mad scheme of yours, I'm really glad not to be part of either."

"Good. As you already have pointed out, I am neither as well. But with you, I am beginning to suspect otherwise. Please Mike, go back to the window, look outside, and marvel at what I've built."

I obliged and looked at the sprawling capitalistic mayhem that seemed to virtually spring up overnight in this part of San Francisco. "Hasn't changed much since the last time I looked."

Again, Jasper ignored my attempt at humor. "These things, this empire I built so far. I've expanded beyond what one man can grasp. I've gotten too big as a legitimate company to handle all of my affairs by myself. And as a legitimate company, I need a face for Hoffman International Investments. I've also been thinking of my legacy. Who can I pass this, all I've built, down to. I have no children, and the woman I was most impressed with, the one who I thought might one day become my wife, well, let's just say you ended her career quite early."

"Who?"

"Laura. Laura Grandviewer."

"Laura," I repeated, remembering the woman who had sent me on a wild goose chase in order for her to confront a black market adversary, and who died at my hands in a shootout.

"I realized at an early age, Mike, that in times of crisis, you sometimes need to step back and take a moment to understand the world around you and the ramifications of your actions and the actions of others. And at that time, I did realize what had happened was nothing personal, and I shouldn't take it that way, but Laura, oh, Laura Grandviewer, she was different. She was special. She had a good head on her shoulders, and for a while, I must admit, I really thought about extracting revenge on you, but then I realized no, you didn't know who you were dealing with, and I thought better. And now I have no one to lean on. Sure, a man of my caliber, my strengths, my ingenuity, and capabilities, you wouldn't think would need one, a woman, a soulmate, one to walk beside me as I begin to make my final push in life, achieve my greatest accomplishment, become the man that I always wished to be. But, yes, although I foresee many more years before me, I wish to lay the groundwork for my design of the future to live on. I already know, once my current plans are in motion, my name will live on. It's just that I wish my plans to continue past my lifetime."

"Ever look into Sinistermatch.com?" I laughed. "Really, you have the money, I'm sure you can buy most anything, or anyone, you want. I mean really, I see you surround yourself with beautiful women and ugly men. Less competition, eh? I must admit, I do like your choice in ordinary secretaries. That Jessica Windrop, and even that front desk woman when I first entered."

"Oh, no, no, no," Jasper assured me. "These are no ordinary secretaries. My employees, those around me, besides being the best in their fields, must come to the table with a particular sort of skill set, a combination of intelligence, values, physical skills, discipline, obedience, and loyalty. However, if they bring just that, they of course will never be my equal. Someone who could now be by my side would have to have greater qualities than all of those I just listed. They would have to have ingenuity, be focused, passionate, and be able to let go of simple sentimentalities. And that, my friend, is hard to come by." Jasper paused for a moment, and then ended with, "That person, the one who will be by my side at the end, who is destined to continue my legacy once I am long gone, she would have to have all of those qualities I just mentioned and even more…or the person who was by my side would have to be of the same blood."

In my mind, without even considering whom I was talking to, or considering the situation, I began to rattle off in my head the qualities Jasper had just mentioned. I could be loyal to my friends, such as Joe and Marilyn and Ozzie. I had skills of sorts to do my job, I considered myself fairly intelligent, not as physical as I once had been, often passionate in what I thought was right, creative when need be, but in the line of values, I already could tell I wouldn't fit into Jasper's organization. And that's when I remembered the Hoffman International Investments organization chart we had found, and the person who I had first asked to see. It wasn't Jasper who was on top, head of the company; there was someone above him, Michael Hoffman.

"So what does your boss think about all of this, your schemes, your black market dealings, your crazy belief that you will use the Occupy Wall Street and Tea Party movement to make you the most powerful man in the world?"

There was silence from the speakers, then an annoyed Jasper asked, "You mean what does Michael Hoffman think of me?"

"Exactly."

"There is no one above me. As I said before, I found that I can no longer manage this company on my own. I need someone by my side. Someone I can trust."

I was still wrapping my head around what Jasper was saying. When I see something written, such as an org chart, it places that information like a message chiseled in stone into my head, while spoken words, on the contrary, are more ethereal.

"So Michael Hoffman isn't really the head of Hoffman International Investments," I stated. "You are."

"As long as I am alive," Jasper affirmed before nearly knocking me out of my seat with what he would say next.

"Mike," Jasper said in solid business-speak. "I've been trying to get your feet wet for quite some time now; sending you offerings, job offers as such, and you keep on refusing. I wanted to start you from a lower level, to bring you in and let you work from the ground up, but unfortunately, you had a way of killing off my emissaries; from Laura Grandviewer to Colin Broadmore."

"I was simply defending myself on both those occasions."

"Mike," Jasper's voice became softer. "This place, the head of this company, this empire I've built, has been reserved for you. Mike, Michael. We can make a great team. With my plans and your no-holds-barred, gung-ho, guns a-blazing attitude, we will make an unstoppable team. And more importantly, who better to look out for you, for your future, as well as my legacy than a family member?"

"What?"

"Mike," Jasper confirmed. "You're my brother. You're my younger brother."

"What?"

Jasper laughed. "Well stepbrother, actually. Brother from a different mother. And I must say, we did have an unusual childhood, didn't we?"

"What?"

"I know this must be a shock to you. Our father told me when I was still young never to contact you. Initially, it was a matter of him wishing to keep his, quote, other family, intact. Your family intact, and my family…well, my family was already broken, but it also went from a wish to a necessity."

10

I ALMOST FELL BACKWARD OUT of my chair, but instead, I shot out of it, raced over to the mirror, and tried to see beyond the glass.

"I have a brother," I heard myself saying aloud.

"And would you be surprised if I told you our father was one of the biggest players in the San Francisco underworld throughout the seventies and early eighties?"

I grabbed my forehead and rubbed my hands to the back of my head. "I don't get it. All this time."

"He was a cop. Worked in the Tenderloin. But of course you knew that. But he did things, met people. Through the course of doing work down there, he also did business. First low level stuff, shakedowns, drug smuggling, and the like. That's how it was in the early seventies. But then he took it to another level, him and a couple of his partners. They expanded, made a network. They were emulating the dons of New York and Chicago. They were family, not of Italian descent, not of blood, but a family of the shield, the silent blue line helped to conceal their activities.

"When I was old enough, old enough and smart enough to make my own decisions, he brought me into his business. And I thrived. Oh, Mike, how I thrived, and I was so smart at my age. I knew where our father was going, but I saw an end to it, and I wanted it to go on and expand, so I invested, diversified, and soon I became too big for our father. He offered me a slice, but I wanted the whole pie. He showed me that with power and strength, you can influence most anyone. And once you had money, nothing could stop you. In the eighties, I established my wealth, so when the bubble blew in the late nineties, I worked on my foundations, strengthening my base, exploring small side ventures as I waited out the storm.

"Understand, Mike? I had grown beyond our father's scope. Indeed, as far back as in the seventies, he read the writing on the wall, and he tried to restart with you, but you rebelled against him. You bucked him. You were too independent, like me. You followed a career in the private investigator business, something he hated as he couldn't control private investigators the way he could fellow officers. Private investigators have no loyalty to each other, or to the badge. That's really why he left you alone. He could never have trusted that you would keep silent, unlike me. I've pulled the trigger only once in my whole life, Mike, and that was under our father's guidance. Since that moment, I could—had—to keep my mouth shut, until at some point, I controlled him. He would— had to—do what I told him. That was probably the same time he left the force. He had become too big, and too big of a liability to remain. A deal was brokered, and he left the force and had to leave town to keep the shame off the city. And he had to leave a budding empire to me.

"But he has never forgotten you, Mike. He asks how you are doing now and again."

"I have a brother. And my father is still alive."

"Mike, on the books, the clean books, we are a multibillion dollar company. Off the books, well, let's just say you can have anything you ever wanted; houses, women, cars. Hell, you can buy a small country if you like. There is so much money to be had; even the most avaricious of men's appetites would be sated. And look what you'll be getting, not only an empire, but your family. Something you've been missing for a good part of your life."

I flopped back in the chair I had called home off and on for the past hour and rubbed my face. My dad still thinks of me. Still worries about me. That asshole. Beat me especially after my mom left. If she left. Maybe she just conveniently disappeared. And now I had a brother as well. And an apparently freaky psycho asshole brother of the highest sorts.

"Jasper, Jasper, Jasper," I said. "You almost had me at the car thing. Look, I don't want anything to do with you or your so-called empire, your plans for world domination, or even anything to do with you or our father. He is part of my past, and you are someone I've never known. I'm just going to take myself out of your office and pretend we never had this meeting."

I headed toward the double doors I had previously been led through, and tried them. They were locked. I gave a sour look back to the mirror.

"You are my younger brother, Mike," Jasper stated. "You leave when I say you can leave. And I guess you already know you can expect me to be calling on your offices to demand the return of information you unjustly stole from me when you hacked into our computers."

"Hey!" I marched back to the mirror, anger welling up in me for a life built on lies. "Why don't you come out from behind the glass. Let's talk as brothers. Face to face. I have a nice chair out here next to mine waiting for you."

"No," Jasper said, calm as ever. "I see that sometimes family, as sometimes friends, do not make good business partners. I am cutting you off. Before we even begin. I thought we would work together, but although we are of the same blood, we are not of the same cloth."

"Didn't you see I was leaving?" I yelled back. "I was calling this off first, before you!" And then I did something childish, something a younger brother might do to his older brother when schoolyard roughhousing gets out of hand: I gave Jasper my best imitation of a Johnny Cash sneer and big middle finger, something I once saw on a poster.

That seemed to do the trick. I heard the intercom click off then back on and then I heard the lock of double doors in the back of the room click.

"I bid you farewell, Mike," Jasper said. "May your future be one of peace, poverty, and boredom."

The Gorilla and Moleman bounded into the conference room through the double doors and rushed toward me and again, sandwiching me between them.

"Take him out," Jasper commanded. "If you need to, make sure his suit is roughed up, but not too much. He is a relation."

As the merry trio consisting of the Gorilla, the Moleman, and myself passed through the double doors, we were met by Jessica Windrop. She was carrying a bottle of Mumm Champagne in one hand, and a pair of champagne glasses in the other.

"I'd tip my hat if I had one and my arms were free," I said.

She responded by harumphing her way around me.

11

WHEN I WAS YOUNGER, maybe even just ten years ago, my ego would have been bruised if I had left Jasper's offices without some contusions. But I am older now, more mature. I decided to wait for a less public location to get into it.

The same beasts that had escorted me through Jasper Hoffman's offices and to the Gallery, the Gorilla and Moleman, now escorted me to the elevator, one on each side, arms looped around mine. Once inside, I shook them off, adjusted my tie, and fixed my hair. They seemed to be fine with that. I then slipped my right hand into my coat pocket, clutched my knuckle brace made by a roll of quarters, and slipped my hand back out as the ape on my right, the one who apparently had learned the button pushing skills the other one lacked, pressed the button for the first floor.

The elevator doors closed and I made a very noticeable movement with my head to look at the floor numbers light up as we began to drop sequentially down. My movement did what I had hoped it would do. It prompted the Gorilla, who was on my left, to lift his head, which gave me the split second I needed.

I took down Moleman by running my heel quickly and forcibly down from his shin to foot, thereby breaking his foot. Then when the Gorilla grabbed at me, I gave him an upper cut with my quarter knuckle brace, knocking him out cold. I then went back to Moleman, and with a swift kick to the jaw, he was out. When I frisked them, I found a gun on the Moleman, which I placed in my pocket.

The elevator doors opened when we reached the first floor and a woman who was about to board the car stopped in her tracks with her mouth open as she saw the two very large men out cold on the floor. I shrugged my shoulders, hit my chest before pretending to burp into my hand, and then pressed the elevator button to return to Jasper's office.

"Bad gas," I said and the woman put a hand over her mouth and stepped back. I held the doors open. "Marilyn!" I called out, "Mr. Hoffman wants to meet you." Marilyn came running as fast as she could in her high heels and carrying my Zap Cane. I waved and nodded that it was OK to the security guard.

Marilyn stopped at entrance of the elevator, staring at the two on the floor.

"Get in," I commanded. And she carefully stepped in.

"She's used to it," I winked to the woman standing outside elevator, still in shock as I wrinkled my nose. Marilyn looked down at the two men as she entered and then up at me with a look of surprise on her face.

"Ape shit," I said.

Marilyn stepped over the Gorilla and kept an eye on both of them as the elevator doors closed. She handed me the cane and I activated the charge.

I knew when we arrived onto the floor of Jasper's offices we would be seen; those television monitors showing the hallway down to the elevator being watched by the steely eyed front desk woman. Perhaps, though, I could catch them off guard.

"Give me a few moments," I told Marilyn. "Just hold the door until I make it down the hall and through the double doors. Be careful, be wary. If you're going to get cold feet, I need to know now and you can go back down, otherwise, I expect you to have my back."

"Darling. I've got your back." Marilyn kissed my forehead as a mother would kiss her child before being sent off to school. "Now do your thang," she said and slapped my butt.

When the elevator doors opened, I immediately ran down the hall holding my Zap Cane in my hand like a spear, until I reached the double doors. I tried to open them and they were locked. I kicked them once, then again, and I could hear the wood around the bolt break. I kicked them one more time and the door cracked open. One run against the doors with my shoulder, and they opened wide. I stopped in my tracks. The secretary was standing up from behind her desk and she was reaching into her hair. I knew something was coming next and I instinctively put up my arm just as she threw a dart that caught me in the hand, causing me to drop my cane.

"Youch!" I yelled in surprised shock, and before I could say anything else, she threw another, then another. I turned, catching one in my shoulder and one in my back. "Fuck!" I screamed, just as Marilyn came barging in and ran around to the side of the table to lunge at my assailant.

As I turned again to face the dart wielding office assistant, I had to pause and watch for a split second because the following sight was so funny. Marilyn, who easily outweighed the assistant two to one, had wrapped one of her legs around the matchstick legs of the assistant and yanked both of them to the ground, falling hard on top of the secretary and pounding her head on the carpet. There's something to be said about brute strength over trained technique.

"Oww, oww!" yelled the secretary, slapping Marilyn in the face with one hand while pushing up on her chin with the other.

Marilyn seemed to let up for a moment, but then retaliated by laying a forearm across the woman's head while fiddling around in her purse with her free hand to grab a stun gun.

"Akkkk!" screamed the secretary as Marilyn zapped her again and again. The second time in the neck.

I pulled the darts out of my hand and shoulder, then pulled off my coat to extract the dart that was in my back. "Enough. Enough," I said to Marilyn as I made my way around to the pair on the floor.

Marilyn was able to zap the woman one more time before I pulled her off.

"And stay down!" Marilyn said, dusting herself off. "Beeatch!"

I went back and grabbed my Zap Cane, and although Marilyn and I were two stunning individuals, with her stun gun and my cane, I knew I had to get a gun to her. "Can you shoot?" I asked.

"Anyone can shoot," Marilyn replied. "You just need to be able to hit what you aim at."

I tossed her the gun I had gotten off the Moleman. I knew she would use it well.

"Get out of the view of the glass and doors," I said to Marilyn as I tried the next set of double doors and opened one wide enough to see some men running down the hall in our direction.

"Shit," I said under my breath as I closed the doors and held my foot against them.

"You always get into it like this?" Marilyn asked.

"Always," I said. "No problem."

The handles on this set of double doors turned and I pulled them back to the lock position. I also held the double doors closed with my foot and shoulder. Someone kept trying the handle and knocking their weight against the doors.

The prone secretary moaned and Marilyn went back to zap her in the neck. I shot Marilyn a look and she shrugged, then stopped in her tracks in reaction to the tapping at one of the panes of glass that bordered the doors.

"Mike," Marilyn called. "Mike!"

I looked around the door and through the glass pane to see one of the men in the hall holding a handgun pointed at Marilyn.

I flipped the switch on my Zap Cane and leaned against it as if I needed it, then nodded to Marilyn to let her know things were about to go down. I then stepped back from the doors, and one flew open.

A thug stepped through the doorway, followed by the one with a gun, while another one stayed beyond the double doors.

I took a step forward and quickly raised the Zap Cane straight to the crotch of the one holding the gun. He immediately dropped the gun as he flew backward through the air and into the guy just beyond the double doors. The young kid who had passed through the threshold first had a look of amazement on his face, which was soon erased as I tapped his leg with the cane.

Zap! Down he went. The guy who had been nearly knocked to the ground when I hit the first guy with the gun scrambled for something inside his suit, a gun, of course. I dropped to the ground and picked up the gun that had been dropped by the first gun-toter. The young man took a couple of panic shots as the door closed. He was ready to run. I knew it, so I shot through one of the glass panes and pointed the gun at him. "Get in here!"

He dropped his gun and followed my commands. Once through the door, I could see he was truly scared, his face ashen white. I motioned to the secretary on the ground. "Go back to school," I told the young kid. "And take her with you."

I looked through the glass pane and down the hall, and a shot rang out, hitting the double doors and creating a little peephole.

"Marilyn, you go, too," I said. "Get out while you can."

"Shit, I ain't going nowhere. I don't know what's behind us." She checked her stun gun and it crackled, still charged. She put it in her purse and slung her purse over her neck like a military knapsack. She checked the gun I passed her and smiled.

I looked though the shattered pane of glass and another shot rang out as I ducked back; this time, the shot just missed me and shattered a television monitor on the far wall above my head.

I jumped away from the doors and shattered glass, taking cover behind the wall. A series of shots rang out and more holes were made in both doors and the walls Marilyn and I were using for cover. I took a couple of breaths, jumped back to the doors, grabbed the door lever, swung it open, and shot three times. A man down at the end of the hall jumped out and fired. I dropped to the floor between the two guys I had zapped earlier with my cane and fired back. The man at the end of the hall spun around and went down. I looked to my left and right then again straight down the I-shaped hallway. I could see some people looking out from offices then ducking back in. These weren't ordinary workers. Most ordinary citizens would stay hidden, under cover. Their looking out meant trouble, and I was about to run into the fire.

I got up and ran for the corner edge of the hall and one of the offices. The guy I had blasted with the Zap Cane to the crotch was now on his hands and knees slowly trying to crawl away. As I ran to retrieve my Zap Cane, which I had again dropped, I used the back of the second guy I had zapped as a springboard. Down he went again, this time face into the tile. He was out. As I headed back to the corner of the hall for protection, I zapped the guy in the crotch who was crawling away a second time. He was now out of commission.

I again peeked down the length of the hall and a pair of men on either end of the hallway poked their heads out and fired. I fired back, then dove toward the two guys on the floor. I patted both of them down, found another gun, and retrieved an extra clip. I then rolled back to the corner of the hallway.

I ditched my Zap Cane, as I now had two guns in my possession, but I was still in a tough position. At any moment, someone could come out from the rooms down the small hall behind me. I needed to check my back.

I looked back through the double doors and could see Marilyn, who had been waiting and watching for my lead. I nodded and aimed down the hall as Marilyn made it in, opposite me.

I pointed to my eyes and then down the hall for Marilyn to keep watch as I checked the short halls and doors that were leaving us the most vulnerable. Down my side was a pair of double doors with a sign over it that read Conference Room A. I tried the doors and they were locked, but that could change at any moment. I continued down the hall to the next door, which was labeled Supplies. This door was unlocked. I opened it, found the regular expected office supplies, and I grabbed some desk staplers. At the double doors marked Conference Room A, I kicked a pair of the staplers into the doorjambs to use as door stoppers. I then made my way back down the hall to opposite Marilyn.

"Door jambs," I said, and tossed a couple of desk staplers in her direction. She picked them up and got to work as I formulated my next move, which was to hopscotch down the long hall from one office to the next, zig zagging across if necessary, making my way to the Gallery and the other side of the mirror, where Jasper Hoffman had been.

When Marilyn returned, I could see perspiration running down her face.

"You OK?" I asked.

"Lead the way," she said, wiping her brow.

"You've seen action movies haven't you?" I asked, and Marilyn nodded.

"Then cover me," I said and made my move to the first office on my side, looking for movement in the office opposite and down the hall as I rushed into the room.

The first office I came to, I found a young petite blonde woman crouched behind her desk.

"Don't hurt me," she pleaded.

"Don't worry," I said. "Either stay put or make a run for it."

"I want out," she cried.

"OK." I extended my hand and that was when she struck, pulling me down with all her weight. I fell over and hit my head on the desk. She then sprung up like a cat, kneed me twice in the side, and tried to hit my head into the desk. I instinctively struck back with my hand holding the gun, striking her on the side of the head. She was out.

And that's when I saw Marilyn making her way into the office on her side of the corridor. Apparently she took it that this was a team event and she was going to clear her side as I cleared my side. I went to my office doorway and gave cover as Marilyn made her way to the office opposite me. Once inside, she looked toward me and motioned that it was my turn to move down the hall to the next office.

That was when she was hit. A small woman came out from hiding behind the door and jumped onto Marilyn's back, one arm around Marilyn's neck in an attempt to choke her out.

Marilyn instinctively dropped her gun, then ran backward into a wall, the back of her head hitting the woman's face, causing the back of the woman's head to hit the wall. The woman let go of Marilyn and dropped like a rag doll to the floor. There was a large indentation in the wall where her head had made contact.

Marilyn dusted herself off, picked up her gun, then motioned, "After you."

I squeezed my lips and made my move to the next office. This time I went straight to checking behind the door and under the desk, but wasn't fast enough to check behind a vertical filing cabinet, and as I was checking under the desk, I heard a man snicker and felt the cold barrel of a gun at the back of my head. I had forgotten what Jasper had mentioned, everyone who worked with him were, in one form or another, trained with special skills, and I now guessed, assassins. I thought it was the end when I heard the shot. It was Marilyn. She had hit my assailant with a dead eye shot as she was making her way to the next office on her side of the corridor. Her shot was destructive, and the man who had the gun on me tumbled backward, dead.

I looked to Marilyn. She shook for a moment, wiped her brow, took a deep breath, quickly cleared the office she just entered, and then motioned with her gun for me to continue.

In the third office I entered, I wasted no time and knocked out a little bespectacled man I found crouched under his desk. I then could only laugh as Marilyn pounced on someone she found hiding in the next office she entered, looking like a wrestler as she used a chair, a filing cabinet, and finally a trash can to subdue the occupant.

We were now near the end of the hallway, and I could hear some rustling. They were making ready for us. I motioned with both hands for Marilyn to stand back, and for the first time, she did.

I poked my head out from the office and had it nearly shot off by automatic fire. Three times I poked my head out like a groundhog in a carnival game, and each time, shots rang out from either side of the end of the hallway.

I waited and wondered if they knew there were two of us. Marilyn had fired only one shot, the shot that had saved me. All of the other shots had been fired by me. I motioned to Marilyn to get behind the desk and that if someone came down the hall, to fire.

A voice crackled over an intercom. It was Jasper. "Come out, Mike. You have no place to go. We're done with the games. We've all had our fun now."

I could hear someone was creeping down the hall and I jumped when Marilyn opened fire, the bullet lodging in a wall, followed by the sound of someone scrambling away from me.

I needed a break to a catch my breath and take hold of the situation. I looked up at the flat-screen television that was showing the undersea nature program and remembered that in each office we had entered, the same nature program was being watched. The robots were now inspecting barnacle encrusted barrels. One of the robots moved closer to one of the barrels, outstretched a robotic arm, and knocked a crab off a barrel.

I looked around the room. On the walls were cartography maps showing the landscape outside of the Golden Gate. Three large swaths were sectioned off with giant red triangles as site 1, site 2, and site 3. Colored pins were within the triangles, some red, some yellow, some black. I surmised that this underwater television show on all the flat screens probably had something to do with these areas marked outside of San Francisco Bay.

There were more rustling sounds coming from down the hall, and I fired a couple of Hail Mary shots in the general direction of where

I heard the noise. Whoever was down there returned fire, shooting wildly, shattering the glass in the office Marilyn was in and spraying the hall with glass. That was when I popped out of my office and fired point blank into a shooter. He dropped just as another shooter appeared at the end of the hallway. He began to fire and I ducked as I returned fire. Marilyn in turn came out and started firing. I'm not sure who shot him or who shot out the window behind him, but when he fell back against it, his gun wildly shooting and finishing the window, he went straight out and to the street below.

Both Marilyn and I looked in stunned astonishment as wind now whipped through the floor, sucking paper out of the offices into a hallway whirlwind.

"Really!" Marilyn said, more as a statement than a question.

"Get back!" I said. "Cover."

Papers were flying out toward the broken window and the roar of wind was deafening. I yelled and ran for the last office on my side. When I hit the open door with my back, I was able to see down the hall toward the Gallery. It was clear, but this last office also put me in a crappy position since the front was all glass, there was virtually no protection.

I quickly scanned the room for potential assailants, as well as for protection. Underneath the desk, I found a bald and bearded man.

"Don't move," I said. "I'll kill you. Like all the others." I was sure this one didn't know what had happened to any of the others, but I was spitting with a dry mouth and he took it for the truth.

"I won't!" he cried.

"Marilyn!" I yelled out over the roar of the wind. "Don't move."

We had been battling our way down the hallway, and seeing how my view from this last office afforded me a view down the lower hall but exposed me to attack, I didn't want Marilyn to encounter a situation she couldn't handle.

"Who's in that last office?" I screamed at the bearded man who was shaking beneath his desk.

"Sergey," he said.

"Tell Sergey to come over here," I commanded. "Tell him he won't get hurt."

The bearded man followed my instructions and Sergey came running. "I'm coming. Don't shoot! Don't shoot!"

"I've killed all your friends and I'll kill you too if you don't obey my orders."

I stepped out of the office and peeked around the corner. It was clear.

"Marilyn!" I called out. "Get over here!"

Marilyn came running, her eyes were wide and wild. She was sweating profusely, her finger on the trigger of the gun.

"Tie these two up."

"Motherfuckers!" Marilyn said and hit both of them with the butt of her gun. She searched them, found a gun on Sergey, then got to work with power cords, monitor cords, an extension cord, a fan cord, and a keyboard to tie them up. It didn't look pretty, but it would slow them down.

As she did this, I was afforded some time between looking down the hall and checking out this office. This office contained some rolled up blueprints that were on the desk. I spread them out and took a quick look. It was a design of something that looked like some sort of engine or motor, but it had two exhaust fans and a tube running to a box that was labeled reservoir.

Through the whipping sound of wind, we could hear the sound of sirens. Police were on the way; our party was soon to be joined.

I got down on one knee and slapped the two restrained men clearly and plainly. "You probably can wiggle your way out, but just listen. If you stay, you're fine. If I see you up and out, you're dead. Understand?"

They both nodded.

"Marilyn," I said. "You OK?"

Marilyn had some blood and bits of glass on her forehead and held a gun in each hand.

"Oh, I'm pumped up now!" she said.

I laughed. "Good. Here's the next move. I need to check down this hall, and I need you to cover me. Keep your guns pointing down the hall toward the door that says Gallery. I'm just going to run down this hall in the opposite direction to make sure our backs are covered, that the doors are secure, OK?"

"OK," Marilyn confirmed she had my back.

Over the rushing of the wind, we could now hear the sound of helicopters joining the police sirens and rescue crews rushing to the building.

I headed down the hall to the right, confident that Marilyn had my back. At the end of the hall was a set of double doors. A sign above the door read Conference Room B. The doors were locked. I met back up with Marilyn.

"OK. We're going to be moving forward down the hall toward that room called the Gallery. I'll keep us covered for whatever appears in front of us. I want you to watch for anything that might come from behind. But be careful, there may be cops coming our way. Be prepared to follow their orders exactly to the T. We're going to walk slowly, almost back to back. OK?"

"OK," Marilyn confirmed.

We made our way down the hall, back to back, and every so often, I would feel Marilyn's rear end prodding me down the hall.

When we arrived at the Gallery, I cautiously opened the doors and we entered. Marilyn was now working on clearing the room like a real professional.

"Mike." A familiar voice crackled over the loudspeaker. "Back so soon?"

I could hear some commotion in the background. "We gotta go. We gotta go," I heard a woman's voice saying.

"Shut up, you stupid bitch!" Jasper screamed.

Marilyn made it to the door near the two-way mirror at the front of the room.

"I wouldn't try anything if I was you," Jasper said. "A couple of my associates and I have our guns trained on you."

"Step back," I said to Marilyn. "Two-way mirror."

Marilyn looked at the mirror, looked back to me, and stepped away, keeping both guns trained at the mirror.

"And who is this friend you have with you?" Jasper asked. "Could this be the Marilyn Jackson I've heard so many complaints about from one of your associates?"

"You must mean Steve," I replied.

"Yes," Jasper said. "So this is the stupid—"

Marilyn gave me a look, and I knew what was going to happen next. I dove for some cover behind the chairs as Marilyn opened fire with both guns blazing at the mirror.

The glass shattered, but there was no returned fire. The room on the other side of the mirror was vacant, save for some green leather couches and chairs, paintings, and what appeared to be a bar. There was also a door on the left side of this observation room.

Laughter rang out on the intercom. Crazed laughter. Jasper was out of control.

I stood up and Marilyn and I headed toward the empty room. We both took a route through the shattered mirror and converged on the heavy door in the back of this observation room.

I checked the door; it was locked from the other side.

"You didn't think it would be that easy, did you?" Jasper laughed.

That was when we heard the explosion.

12

THE EXPLOSION CAME FROM the end of the hallway we had slowly worked through, and I immediately knew it was a flash grenade. "Federal agents!" We could hear commands being yelled. "Drop your guns! Hands in the air!"

We could hear some scrambling, a whirling noise, and then silence from the other side of the wall beyond this last locked door. Jasper was trying to make his getaway. I started kicking the locked door, but it was solid, some sort of heavy oak, and I guessed it was probably more than a simple bolt keeping it locked solid.

"Here," I said to Marilyn. "Hand me your guns."

Marilyn obliged, and I placed them along with the one I had borrowed from one of Jasper's henchmen behind some bottles in the bar. I checked the bottles of booze, found Bullet whiskey, and fixed myself a glass as Marilyn watched with a look of fright and amazement. I raised a glass. "What can I make you?"

"What are we going to do?" Marilyn pleaded for an escape.

"What can we do?" I said. We continued to hear shouts and commands, a couple of gunshots. The agents were making their way to us. "Sure?" I raised my glass.

"Make mine a double," Marilyn said as she sat down in one of the plush green leather chairs. "Make it sweet."

I poured some cranberry juice in a martini glass, added some Grey Goose vodka, and stirred it. I brought Marilyn her drink, we toasted, and I sat down in another chair as random shards of glass from the broken mirror continued to fall.

"I'm scared," Marilyn confided.

"Don't be," I smiled. "Everything will be all right. Just don't make any sudden moves and follow their orders. I'll try to keep their attention on me, keep the heat off of you."

Suddenly, a gaggle of agents wearing black tactical gear burst in through the same Gallery double doors that Marilyn and I had come through earlier, automatic guns drawn, pointing this way and that, barking commands, and making their way cautiously to the frame of what was once a two-way mirror. These agents were followed by a trio wearing suits. One of the agents wearing a suit started squawking to the throng and told them to hold position as he made his way to the front of the pack.

Marilyn had done well, following their commands, dropping her drink and getting on her hands and knees, arms raised in the air. And I did as I had promised; I just sat there, slowly taking another drink, with most of the guns trained on me.

When the agent from the back of the pack arrived at the front, I immediately recognized him as Cory Rodgers.

I had met Cory Rodgers a couple of years back, when he was just a pimply faced newbie in the Agency. I had sort of taken advantage of him back then. Actually, I'd made him look a little foolish, with Joe eventually having to step in to smooth everything out.

There was a big grin on Cory's face as he stepped through the window frame to stand in front of me. "You son of a bitch!" Cory cursed, and slugged me across the chin.

It was a pretty good hit but the strength and power behind it wasn't impressive. I didn't even drop my drink. I just rubbed my chin, not wanting Cory to get the better of me. "Nice to see you, too," I said and fixed my hair with my free hand. "What brings you here?"

"Who's behind that door?" Cory yelled, spittle flying from his mouth as he motioned to the door in the back of this observation room.

"Your guess is as good as mine."

Cory commanded a couple of agents to try the door that I had failed to get through, and they failed as well. "Open up!" they started yelling, "Federal agents!"

There was no response.

"Get through it!" Cory ordered.

Shots were fired at the lock and the door didn't open. One of the agents, with a name tag reading Frank sewn above the right breast pocket of his bulletproof gear, called up a battering ram. A half dozen more agents showed up carrying a heavy looking black cylinder with handles. They used this on the door and finally one of the panels on the door splintered. Another hit resulted in an opening being made that was just large enough for a flash grenade to be tossed into the next room.

There was an explosion and the door shook, but it didn't burst open. The agent named Frank ordered one of his comrades to reach through the hole that had been made in the door, and after fiddling around a bit, he hollered, "Got it."

Another agent kicked open the door, and as smoke billowed out, the half dozen agents dressed in tactical gear, looking very much like Canadian geese, began dodging and weaving their way into the room. Our room was partially filled with smoke, and then quickly emptied as it was sucked out through the broken window in the hallway.

"Clear!" one of the agents yelled from the back room.

"What do you see?" Cory called out, giving me a smirk as if he was about to find something back there that would incriminate me more than whatever he currently thought he had on me.

"Nothing."

"What?" Cory said. "You certain?"

"Nothing," said the agent named Frank as he exited that back room. "The room is literally empty."

"What?" Cory said, as he rushed over to investigate the room himself. He stood in the doorway, pulled out a handkerchief to cover his nose and mouth, and disappeared in the back for just a moment before coming back out to face me.

"Was he back there?"

"Who?"

"You know who."

"I don't have the slightest idea what you're talking about."

"Oh, come on," Cory said. "Enough with the games already. We've been watching this place from across the street and when I saw you come into the building, I knew things probably would be going down in some way today. Just didn't figure you'd force us to blow our cover."

I thought about that for a moment and then started laughing.

"What's so funny?" Cory asked.

"Have you been sitting in that Wardrobe on Wheels out front?"

Cory blushed and I knew that was where he had been leading his surveillance team.

I also noticed the agent named Frank had moved away from the other agents who were still on high alert, pointing their guns at Marilyn and myself and any inanimate object that apparently looked threatening. Though I wasn't sure where he stood in the hierarchy of things, I took it that Frank carried some authority here, and it seemed that he liked seeing Cory in a bind. A big smile crossed his face when I made that comment about the Wardrobe on Wheels.

I laughed even harder. "Cory, I never thought of you as a lady's man! Or a man who liked woman's lingerie!"

That broke Frank, and Cory's face twisted. He was mad and embarrassed and responded by going after Marilyn. He motioned to his suited cohorts to grab her. They did a quick pat down, put on handcuffs, and pulled her up to her feet. "Take her outside!" Cory commanded.

"Don't worry, Marilyn," I yelled as they took her away. "Everything's going to be all right."

This prompted a couple of tactical agents to converge upon me, guns to my head.

"Should we frisk him?" one of them asked of Cory, and then looked to Frank.

"Yeah, sure," Cory said. "Although it looks like he's done damage here, I doubt you'll find anything on him."

"You know me too well," I assured him.

One of the agents knocked the empty glass out of my hands and pulled me out of my chair by the lapels, while the others kept their guns trained on me. I was thoroughly frisked, and it took me a moment to straighten myself back out when they were done.

"Mind if I take a look?" I asked, motioning toward the back room.

"Sure," Cory said. "It's empty."

I walked to the back room and was followed by the agent named Frank. I checked the door, the latch, and the bolt that had securely locked the door. It had to have been locked from the inside. There appeared to be no other way in or out of the room. I tapped the walls, and they were solid, strong. They felt as if they were made of cement, not plaster and sheetrock. The floor was tiled, as was the ceiling. It was a secure room, a safe room, where a person or persons could retreat to if something was going down. And it was completely empty.

"Remind me, how many floors does Hoffman International Investments take up in this building?" I asked agent Frank who had been staying right behind me as I inspected the room.

"Just one? This one?"

"Yes."

"And the floor above, below?" I asked.

"Vacant," he stated and gave a cold stare to another agent in the room.

This agent picked up the cue and began to stomp heavily on the individual tiles on the floor. He was quickly joined by all the others in the room. I continued checking the walls until I reached the end of the room and the back wall. It too was made of cement or the like. I then began scanning the ceiling until I came across one of the four by four ceiling tiles that appeared a little cockeyed.

"What's that?" I pointed up to the ceiling.

"Get me up there," Frank commanded.

Two agents came together, interlocked their hands, and hoisted agent Frank up to the ceiling. He pulled a utility tool from his belt and worked a corner of the tile. Once he was able to work a finger underneath it, he replaced his utility tool and pulled out a looping wire from his belt. He then slid the wire under the corner of the tile.

"Drop!" he yelled, and the two agents stepped back. The tile on the ceiling dropped about a foot. Metal tubing and a cable of some sort could be seen connected to the tile and disappearing deep into the recesses of the ceiling.

"Give me a hand!" Frank yelled as he dangled and a trio of agents joined in pulling down the ceiling tile.

"It's an elevator of some sort to the floor above!" yelled Frank. "You, you, you, and you!" he commanded, pointing to the agents who helped pull down the tile, "Go up that way! We'll meet you above."

Frank then rushed out of the safe room, followed by the remaining agents. I paused at the doorway to watch the other agents disappear into the recesses of the ceiling above.

"There's an elevator in there," Frank screamed at Cory. "He's making his escape to the floor above. Rodriquez, Gomez, Mack!" Frank called out to his men, "You follow up through the elevator back there, the rest of you, follow me."

"And you," Frank said to Cory. "You just sit here and watch him."

The remaining tactical agents followed agent Frank out of the room in a V formation, leaving me and Cory by ourselves.

"Mind if I get another drink?" I asked Cory as I made my way to the bar. I was planning on making myself a drink whether he said I could or not. As I headed over to set myself up, I could see Cory was crushed, upset, and confused. He was still young, trying to make a name for himself in the Agency, but he was still a novice, still making mistakes. His hitting me across the jaw was not just something that he wanted to do, it was something he had to do to instill his leadership qualities within his ranks.

I poured half a glass of Bullet and added a splash of water.

"You want to know what I think?" I asked as I swirled the liquid in my glass.

Cory shrugged a shoulder.

"I think you're being usurped."

Cory just looked away, embarrassed. He knew it was true, and while he wrestled with the idea of his changing position within his ranks, I reached down into the ice bucket, pulled out one of the guns I had stashed, and pointed it at Cory. He didn't notice.

I took a generous swig of my drink and then came out from behind the bar, gun still pointed at Cory. He finally turned, and his eyes opened wide.

"Never take your eyes off your quarry," I said, "No matter what's going through your mind."

I moved in to within arm's length, gun aimed at his chest, drink in my other hand.

"OK," I said, "What's going on here? Why have you been watching this place, this company?"

"Classified," Cory said. "But it is safe to say it involves national security. And you just fucked everything up."

I took another swig of my drink. From what Jasper had told me, and what I had seen, Jasper was a scoundrel, a billionaire thief, and a madman with dreams of world domination mixed in with some bizarre fascination with underwater archeology. I surmised national security issues were mixed in with at least a couple of my observations.

"I fucked everything up?" I questioned. "I just came here to ask some simple questions; it's not my fault that everyone overreacted."

Another piece of broken mirror fell to the floor and shattered.

Cory just stood there dumbfounded, and still quite aware of the gun pointing at him.

"OK," I continued. "Our computers were hacked and we traced the hack as coming from here, this building, this company. We just dropped by to confront the perpetrators and were treated as unwelcomed guests."

"Looks like it was some confrontation."

"Well, there have also been some overt threats made against me from someone who works here, for quite some time. The boss of this company."

"Michael Hoffman," Cory concluded.

"There's no Michael Hoffman," I informed Cory. "Jasper Hoffman has been running the show. Always had."

"No Michael Hoffman?" Cory was stunned. I could see the wheels turning in his head. His eyes were looking up toward the ceiling as he was putting the pieces together of what he and his agency had uncovered about Hoffman Investments.

"Now, ready to have your mind blown?" I asked, and Cory dumbfoundedly nodded.

"Although there is no Michael Hoffman, Jasper does have a brother. And you know him."

Cory was about to say "oh" and curse, but I broke in with, "Yeah, he's my brother."

Cory was visibly shaken and had to find himself a chair. "Jasper Hoffman, I mean, Jasper Mason," Cory said, and then it was as if a light bulb went off in his head. "How...how are you related?"

"We're stepbrothers. Or at least that's what the man says."

I could see we were now getting onto the same wavelength. I could be of invaluable help to Cory if he worked things the right way, and I would get out of this current mess, if he treated me right. How he treated me, and how we played together, could be a career changer for him and a jail saver for me. It all depended on how he played the hand I had just dealt.

I ejected the clip from the gun I was holding, checked the chamber, and handed the gun over to Cory who remained sitting.

"Why, why, this changes everything," he said, still quite dumbfounded. "Now we know he has a history, a past."

"What history, what past?" I asked. "I just met him myself."

"No, I mean before, we thought the Hoffman brothers, Michael and Jasper were European, probably German or something. They certainly have some strong connections over there. But now things make sense. Michael Hoffman was Jasper all the time. And we just didn't know, I mean that this figure, this guy, this Michael or Jasper, was home grown. And now, from here! Right here in the Bay Area! And he has a relative we can squeeze for information. You! This is a major breakthrough. This turns everything in our investigation on its head."

Cory was shaking his head and swinging the empty gun between his legs. He began muttering, "God. I didn't know! We didn't know! How...who...what..."

I came up alongside Cory and put a hand on his shoulder, "Listen!" I said. "I really know absolutely nothing about Jasper. I just found out myself today that I had a stepbrother and that it was him. I really..." but I didn't finish my sentence. There was a large explosion down the hall, followed by series of smaller ones. Cory jumped out of his chair and grabbed me by the arm just as Frank came running in along with two other agents.

"A fire started in that room over there that looks like a laboratory. The sprinklers aren't coming on and the whole place may go up! We need to evacuate the rest of the building."

"Did you catch him?" Cory asked.

"Not yet. I think he got away."

Cory looked at me then slugged me again, this time with more force. He then pulled out some handcuffs from his waistband and slapped them on my wrists.

"All right," I said. "I'll let you have that one, too. But I'm keeping track."

Cory tried to manhandle me, but I shrugged him off, and he knew better than to press his luck. As we walked along the hallway that Marilyn and I had fought our way down, smoke rushed over our heads and out the broken hallway window. I also noticed multiple fires burning in nearly every office, and the blueprints that I had seen earlier were now missing.

WEEK IV

13

I T HAD BEEN A week since I confronted Jasper Mason, my stepbrother, and a week since Cory and federal agents had burst into the McNamara, arrested, and subsequently released me. The fire at the McNamara had been devastating to the building itself, and it would probably take a couple of months before it was fully reopened. There were pending charges, but as there was plenty of classified documents that would undoubtedly come out in a trail, as my legal team from Naklowycz and Howes pointed out to the agents who had me under their care, things would most assuredly be swept under the rug. It was also understood that since I had been identified as a close relative of Jasper Mason, I would be under intense scrutiny for quite some time; meaning I would be watched from now on.

It also had been a week since I'd heard from Marilyn. I'd gone to her apartment and left her messages, both at work and at her home. In my meetings with the federal agents and my lawyers, her name was brought up, but her situation was unclear, so I figured she was still

133

being held. So I had Joe contact the one person I knew would know of her whereabouts, Cory Rodgers, and once again, Joe would act as a mediator between me and Cory.

The meeting place Joe had arranged was John's Grill over on Ellis Street. It's one of those places of dark wood and photographs of the city of San Francisco and its famous residents. The bar, though well stocked, is the size of a shoe, so we opted for a booth under a cadre of old photographs in a corner, secluded and walled on three sides.

We had just ordered our drinks, a Sidecar for me and gin and tonic for Joe, when Cory waltzed in.

"So where's Marilyn?" I asked, even before Cory had a chance to sit down.

Cory didn't seem to be in his happy place. He looked as if he had been wearing the same suit for the past couple of days. When our drinks arrived, Cory ordered a glass of Cabernet.

"She's still being held," Cory said. "There was an incident while she was being processed."

"By being processed, you mean while she was being taken into custody, she took offense to something your folks were doing?" Joe asked.

"She was in the process of being strip searched," Cory said. "And she took down one of the agents."

I took a sip of my Sidecar to hide my smile, but I was still grinning when I put my glass down. Cory saw that I was smiling and added, "She is now charged with battery."

I laughed as I could picture in my head how that happened, and also I laughed in relief. She was still in their custody, and the reason she was in custody was the person she had taken down was pissed off and was being pacified by his or her superiors holding her. Cory laughed with me, but for his own reasons. However, I'm sure we had now broken the ice between us.

"I'm taking a lot of heat," Cory said. "For everything blowing up on my watch."

"I thought you were going to be looking good for finding out about Jasper's history, about him being my relative."

"That only went so far."

"What about everything in their offices, paperwork, computers?"

"The computers were basically wiped clean of all data and their hard drives destroyed. Someone in their office kicked off a computer program of some sort that first encrypted and then wiped the hard drives clean. It then released a small vial of some sort of acid that had been installed in each of their computers. These vials burst and melted the computer's interiors. That's also what started all the little fires in the building and why you aren't being charged with multiple counts of arson."

"Did they ever find out the reason why the sprinklers didn't come on?" Joe asked, as that had been pointedly remarked about in the news reports that followed the fire.

"The piping on that floor had been cinched shut. Had to have been done by the residents, someone in Hoffman's employ who had done that."

"OK, so beyond some creative computer destruction and building plumbing, why are you after this company and Jasper?" Joe asked, "What do you have on 'em? Why is he on the federal government's radar?

Cory looked over his shoulder to make sure nobody was listening, and then leaned forward. "Jasper Hoffman, or now Jasper Mason, if you will..." Cory said, nodding in my direction, "first came to our attention a couple of years ago. Probably about the same time you and I first met."

Cory leaned back into his seat and took a slow sip and swirl of his glass of Cabernet as he worked out in his head what he was about to tell us next.

"And?" I asked when I couldn't wait any longer.

"What do you know about the state of Georgia?"

"That it's down south," I replied.

"I didn't mean the US state," Cory said, satisfied that I fell for his little trap and joke. "I meant what do you know about the country named Georgia?"

"Wasn't it one of those countries that came about after the fall of the Soviet Union?"

"Exactly. Georgia is one of those."

"Remember that scene in the first Star Wars movie, at the bar, when Luke Skywalker first meets Hans Solo? The whole country of Georgia is like that. It is the wild west of the former Eastern Bloc. Anything can be had for the right amount of money, and everyone is scrambling to make money any way they can. And one of the thriving black markets over there deals with radioactive materials."

"What types are we talking about," Joe asked. "Dirty bomb or nuclear bomb grade?"

"Both," Cory said. "You can get both. Leftovers from the Cold War. The US government along with their European allies have spent billions of dollars trying to secure the sources of these nuclear materials, uranium, plutonium, iridium, europium, cesium, what have you, and even with all their efforts, the black market of these materials is thriving."

"From what I've heard, we've been forced to have the foxes guard the henhouses," Joe remarked.

"Basically," Cory said. "So the United States helped to create and fund a special nuclear police unit back in 2005, which has been operating and successful in setting up stings and the like to get potential threats off the streets. That was all that was being proved until a couple of years ago when we had some buyers come into Georgia actively looking to purchase dirty bomb materials. Well, we got 'em, for a time, before they were assassinated while they were being held in custody in Georgia. But before they were knocked off, that special nuclear police unit was able to extract some important information that led to a financier named Michael Hoffman."

"The same…"

"The same," Cory assured me. "The same, in reality, Jasper Hoffman, or Jasper Mason, if you will. He has attempted several purchases since then, but each time, at least the times we know about, he's been shut out. Through these other attempts, all of which, mind you, ended up with the couriers who were attempting to purchase the goods winding up dead, we would find out a little more about Michael Hoffman, and eventually the name of the company for which he works, Hoffman International Investments."

"So why haven't you just busted him?"

"Lack of evidence, trying to understand his or his company's organization, motivations, intent. We finally got a foothold, a mole within his organization within the past six months."

It then clicked. "Jessica Windrop?"

Cory's face twisted. He wasn't expecting that I knew her.

"Who's Jessica Windrop?" Cory attempted to feign ignorance, but I could see right through him, as did Joe. He was just protecting another agent.

"Nobody," I said. "I just spoke out of line."

Cory's eyes darted back and forth between me and Joe and he sat up stiffly. I emptied my glass and ordered a round for the table. This time, Cory ordered a shot of whiskey.

"We have something for you. Something you'll find of great interest," I confided. "But we'll need something in return."

"What do you have, and what do you want?" Cory asked.

"I like him," Joe said of Cory. "A straight shooter."

"We want Marilyn released, and all charges against me, as well as her, dropped."

"That's a tall order," Cory said, although I knew he could do the part about her being released right off the bat. "What do I get in return?"

"Everything," I said.

"Everything?" Cory looked perplexed.

"Everything," I said. "Everything you ever wanted to know or get from Jasper. The company, documents, encrypted and unencrypted, in English and foreign languages. Everything they had on their computers."

"I told you, their computers are toast," Cory replied.

"Yeah, well, I told you we were hacked, didn't I?"

Cory nodded.

"Well, we have some experts ourselves," I said without mentioning Ozzie. "And we just happened to hack right back into Hoffman International and downloaded anything and everything we could off of their computers, encrypted or not. We saved that data off site. If we gave you all of that information, sure, it will take you a while to sift through, but I think it would put you back in the good graces of your bosses, don't you think?"

Cory responded as I expected, not wanting to give up anything. "Remember the Patriot Act?" he said. "There are things now, ways that we can piece things together, or just go after you and your cohorts directly to get what we want."

"Yes," Joe piped in. "But it won't be easy."

"I wouldn't say that necessarily," Cory replied. "It just so happens that we picked up another one of your cohorts just yesterday, an Ozzie Ferris."

I glanced at Joe, but he gave off an air of indifference.

"And we can delay your investigations by destroying what we have."

Cory responded by tossing in his last card, "You would do that even if it involves national security? And could affect the lives of millions of Americans?"

"My life," I said. "And both of my friend's lives are what is important to me right this second…other things, it depends on the situation."

"I really can make it hard on you guys," Cory said.

"Yeah, well," Joe added. "Do you want to move up, or do you want to be the guy who blew an operation twice."

"Look," I said. "I can give you everything, or I can give information to you bit by bit, as it fits my needs, or you can walk away with nothing. I'm actually giving you everything; the whole kit and caboodle. And truth is, it's really too much data for us to sift through and I don't know what we would be looking for or what to do with it afterward; outside of using it to twist your arm now and again."

Our drinks arrived and Cory took his down in one gulp.

"Look," I said. "I admit, I'm way over my head and we are looking to you, Big Brother, to make things right. So just tell me. Deal? You get everything. Everything that was on their computers."

Cory spun his empty glass and looked at me squarely, "All right. All right!" he said, reaching over the table to shake our hands. "Deal!"

"I want both Marilyn and Ozzie out now, immediately."

"She'll be out by Friday."

"Now!" I demanded. "And Ozzie too!"

"Friday is the best I can do for Marilyn," Cory said. "If it was up to me, she'd be out yesterday. Everything is political, like it or not, even in a place that is supposed to be apolitical. And Ozzie, well, that's another story. He is actually really a whiz kid. Him and some of his buddies. Just talking to him, he's blowing some of our folk's minds. He's not being held, mind you, he is more being interviewed. We think there might be a job for him somewhere within the Agency."

I looked to Joe and Joe looked back at me. "I'll believe it when I see it."

14

POSEIDON WAS THE FIRST to hear the intruder. He awoke me from sleep via a deep growl and moving to the center of my bed. I rubbed my eyes, but since I had been asleep in total darkness, I couldn't see anything in the room. I listened though and there was someone climbing the stairs toward my bedroom. Poseidon continued to growl. It's an old townhouse. I knew if I climbed out of bed, the intruder would hear my movements. I quietly extended my arm to reach for my nightstand drawer, and slowly, quietly, began opening it.

Poseidon went silent. His back was arched, his tail making quick twitching movements. The bedroom door handle turned as my hand found my gun. Poseidon's back feet began to step in place, his butt moving side to side. He hissed. The door creaked open and I pulled my gun from the drawer to aim at the opening door, but I was too late. Poseidon made his move.

In an astounding series of aerobatic maneuvers that I've seen before when he hunts, Poseidon leapt from my bed, catapulted from the bed's baseboard, and hurled himself at the intruder. Cat hisses and cries and human screams intermingled as the intruder hurled himself against the hallway wall, grabbing and screaming at Poseidon, who locked onto his face and chest with claws and teeth. Together they both fell backward down the stairs.

I jumped out of my bed and ran to my bedroom door to stand upon the top landing. For a few seconds, I caught a comical scene that I won't soon forget. At the bottom of the stairs, Poseidon and the intruder were having a face-off; the man on his knees, his right hand cradling the right side of his face around his eye, his left hand alternating between swatting at Poseidon and trying to steady himself.

Poseidon, for his part, was in the classic Halloween cat pose, tail standing tall and stiff, back arched. He was alternating between growls and hisses and swatting back at the man's hand.

"Had enough?" I yelled just as a second intruder showed up to help the man up.

They both looked up toward me; the man on the floor still covering his right eye, and the new man aiming a gun in my direction. I fell backward just as he let a couple of shots fly. I fired back over the landing but I could here them running, making their way toward the back of my place.

I ran down the stairs in pursuit, and when I reached the kitchen, I was overcome by the smell of gasoline. The smell was everywhere and I could see my place was doused in it. And that was when I saw it. At first, it was like a meteor shower, but instead of rushing across the sky, they were coming over the fence, toward my kitchen through the open slider, and directly at me—Molotov cocktails.

My kitchen exploded behind me as I made my way to the living room. I was blown to the floor by the initial explosion and fire. I rushed to the front door just as Poseidon came out from under the living room couch, hot on my heels.

When I opened the front door, Poseidon dashed around me and into the darkness. I went about banging on the neighbor's doors, yelling "Fire! Fire!"

As I was doing this, I just happened to glance over my shoulder and saw a white van skidding out of our complex and speeding down the street. The passenger of the van was dressed in black, and shot wildly in my direction as it sped by.

I hit all of my neighbor's doors and then headed out back, as I didn't wish to remain at the front of the complex in case the van returned. Cathy soon joined me in the back Commons area with her dog Rover. Cathy was wearing a robe and curlers and was crying on my shoulder when I saw Poseidon far down the walkway that lines the back of the townhouses. He was in the hedges. I excused myself from Cathy, gathered up Poseidon, and returned to Cathy's side. The flames were taking over my place, coming out the back patio and now making their way across the living room ceiling.

Poseidon couldn't take it and made his way out of my arms to sit by my side. Rover wasn't as calm and tried to make his way from Cathy, around my legs, and to Poseidon, who responded with a hiss and slap.

"This isn't exactly what I meant when I said I'd have you back for another barbeque," I said to Cathy as the flames licked through my patio and up to my second floor windows. Cathy just sobbed harder into my shoulder. Sometimes jokes, no matter how good the intent, are just not funny.

When the fire department arrived, my place was already fully engulfed. Smoke could be seen billowing out of the second floor windows, and flames were burning their way through the wall my unit shared with Cathy's unit.

From the radio chatter and firemen talking, I learned that not only my place had been hit that night, but actually several places were currently in flames. The Pacifica Fire Department had to call out for mutual aid as the department had shrunk over the years with cut back on their numbers. There were three fires running at once, it was more than they could handle.

I quickly realized that Joe's house had also been hit, so I squeezed Cathy and told her I'd be back as soon as possible, as I had to check in on Joe. I swooped up Poseidon, tossed him into the back of my car, and headed over to Joe's place.

Poseidon made his way to the front, put his front paws on the dashboard, and started howling like a firetruck himself. He was freaking out.

When I arrived at Joe's place, I found more police officers than firemen. Joe was in the process of being grilled by Tony Chin of the Pacifica Police Department. Joe was sitting in the back of a patrol car.

"Ha. Ha," Tony said, and not as a laugh. "So funny strange to see you show up at the place of a murder."

"It was no murder," Joe snapped back from the open window. "I just stood my ground."

"Can I speak to him alone?"

"Are you his lawyer?" Tony asked.

"Is he under arrest?"

"No. Not yet. We are still investigating."

"Then can I speak to my friend in private?"

"Sure," Tony said. He opened the back door of a police car. "Make yourself comfortable."

I closed the door and leaned against it. "What happened?" I asked Joe.

"Well, they were professionals," Joe said.

"How can you tell?"

"Well they somehow were able to disable my alarm system, the one that I pay thirty-five bucks a month for, but they didn't know about the simple motion detectors I have set around the house. When I heard those, I got up real fast."

"How many?" I asked.

"Two," Joe said. "Got one of 'em with both barrels. He's still inside."

We looked toward Joe's place. It was still smoking and firemen were entering and exiting the place but didn't seem to be any real hurry. Crews were also still dousing the place with gallons of water. His place wasn't burned as much as mine.

"When I chased the other one outside, I found I was facing three more by a van. They started hurling Molotov cocktails. Between dodging them, I let off a couple more rounds. Maybe hit one of 'em. In any event, they took off after that real fast."

"So probably the same guys who came after me went after you. Or there was a second team."

"You OK?" Joe asked.

"I think my place is definitely worse off than yours," I said. "But I got one of 'em as well. Or at least Poseidon did. All claws." I made the motion of cat claws with my hands.

"That's some cat," Joe remarked. A fireman on the second floor of Joe's place broke a window with the butt of his ax, which signaled hose men to aim a stream of water in that vicinity.

"You think..."

"Yeah. Probably," Joe said, finishing my thought. "I'm sure they probably hit our Pacifica office, as well as our places in the city. I heard on the radio a structure was burning in the Linda Mar Shopping

Center, so I'm sure they hit it. And if they haven't hit our places in the city, they're on their way."

"Want me to run over?"

"At this point," Joe said, "there's nothing you would be able to do. You have your phone? We need to give a head's up to the SFPD. Have them check our offices and to watch Marilyn's and Ozzie's place. You have the number to the Tenderloin police station?" "Naw," I said. """ I looked at Joe as I dialed 911. Joe was looking dejected. I wanted to say something to cheer him up, but the only thing I could think of was that this was Jasper's way of hitting us back for taking his operation down.

"Yeah," Joe agreed. "And I fear this is a sign that he could get us, anytime, anywhere."

15

JOE HAD BEEN CORRECT, all of our offices had been hit and were burned to one degree or another, with the Tenderloin office having been hit the worst, the resulting explosion raining debris across the street and onto the Tenderloin police station. All of our homes had been hit as well. On the news it was reported that a suspicious fire had burned an apartment in the Tenderloin, that apartment being Marilyn's, and a gas explosion was being investigated in the Bernal Heights district, that being Ozzie's place.

Fortunately, no one had been hurt in any of the attacks, since Marilyn and Ozzie were still being held by the Feds.

"I'm thinking about retiring," Joe said. "For good."

We were sifting though the ashes of our Pacifica Linda Mar office. The police yellow tape was still up as it was an active investigation, but both Joe and I knew they wouldn't find any more than what we already knew, so we just broke the tape and walked inside.

The smell was unmistakable and nearly unbearable, the acrid smoke smell with a hit of gasoline. I checked what was once my desk. It was hard to open the drawers, warped by fire and water. All that had been inside them were in cinders. On the floor near the back wall where Joe had installed my rack of canes, I found the metal frame. It was blackened, and all but one of the canes had been completely burned.

"Retiring? What for? What will you do with all the time on your hands?" I asked as I continued sifting through the ashes—sifting through our past.

Joe didn't answer me directly for his reasons for wanting to retire. Instead he started with, "Marilyn is under the impression that your father was somehow involved in the death of my father. I don't hold it against you, just so you know. What happened between them has nothing to do with us."

"She didn't mention that to me," I said. "She just mentioned that she had tracked down Roosevelt Jones, a potential eyewitness to his murder. Hadn't said anything about my father being involved."

"Well, lookie here." Joe picked up a gold coin, one that he had found on the beach not far from here.

I stepped over to where Joe was standing and he passed the coin to me. "Thinking about going on more hunts for gold?" I asked.

"Maybe complete my next book." Joe had been toying with the thought of retirement, walking the line from semi to full for quite some time now, but these fires, and the thing about his dad and my dad just pushed him over the edge, though he'd never admit to it.

"We'll need to arrange some things. If you want to keep the name, Coastside Detectives, if you want to stay in the business."

"Not sure," I said. "Might be time to look into doing something else."

"Like what?"

"Well, like first off, I have to find a place to stay."

"I have a friend who lives out over in Shelter Cove," Joe offered. "He can probably put you up for a while. He's rarely there and has me drop by to watch it. Maybe he'd want to take you in as sort of like an innkeeper."

"Where's that?"

"Shelter Cove? Out over on San Pedro Point. Just follow the main road up until you can't go any further. There's a long set of stairs from the hilltop down to the places on the beach. Check it out. Let me know."

"Yeah, I will. Definitely."

"Well, whatever you choose to do, workwise," Joe said, "just know I'll always have your back."

"Likewise."

"I think you have a good crew now," Joe said. "You have the tech guru, Ozzie, to watch over the electronics, the street smart Marilyn office manager, and you have yourself, the veteran who knows the business. I'm really not needed anymore."

"Hardly. You have the most valuable commodity, experience."

"Experience enough to know when it is truly time to retire."

"And do what? Sit in your house all day?"

"I have things to do. The Moose Lodge and stuff. And I still have my cabin. Can spend more time up there."

"I thought you sold your place up in Inverness?"

"Almost did. Twice."

"Thinking of moving?"

"No, I think I'll stay put in my place here. Maybe work on my memoirs. Maybe run for local office."

"Politics?"

"Yeah, maybe. What I've seen over the past few years just yanks my chain. Motivates me to want to do something."

"Another hobby."

Joe laughed. "Maybe."

I passed the coin back to Joe. He flicked it with his thumb into the air and caught it. "Maybe I'll just flip a coin to decide what I'll do."

I watched Joe walk away from the ashes that was once our Pacifica branch of Coastside Detectives and into the morning sunlight. His shoulders were hunched and he looked older than I'd ever seen him before, worn out. Retirement. I always thought it would be a relief for whoever decided it was time to go, that they were now released from the constraints of work, but seeing Joe walk off this way, it looked like he was beaten, and about to face a new burden, that of the unknown.

After Joe left, I decided to make my way across Highway One to Shelter Cove as I was, indeed, still in need of a place to stay.

Shelter Cove was a resort destination back when the old Ocean Shore Railroad ran along the coast from San Francisco. From old photographs I had seen, it was at that time a very popular destination where sunbathers could frolic in relatively calm waters and if need be, even rent a room and spend a couple of nights. After the collapse of the railroad, the homes and hotel fell into general disrepair and were largely forgotten by those outside of Pacifica.

Since the only drivable road to Shelter Cove, along Shelter Cove and Shoreline Drive, washed out years ago, the residents of this hamlet have been left with parking high above their community and taking a long nearly vertical hike down to their residences. This in turn resulted in my planned five minute trip following San Pedro Road to where it ends at Kent road taking an additional twenty minutes just to find a parking spot several blocks away, and then hiking to the crest above Shelter Cove.

Standing above this tiny community and looking out at the Pacific Ocean, I could see how the residents reveled in their hermitage lifestyle. It was a clear blue sky with a complementary blue ocean. The crescent shaped cove that backs San Pedro Mountain, in which the community is situated, seems to be in the right spot to be blocked from pounding ocean waves, making the beach there quite tame.

Looking down upon the dilapidated homes and hotel, one would expect a city would red flag them for unsafe living conditions or health and safety hazards, or that the Coastal Commission would fine owners for probable septic systems leaking raw sewage into the ocean, or for limiting public access to a historically public area. Here though, the residents have been able to fend off any governmental or civic attempts to extract them from their idyllic, yet challenging, homesteads. Somehow, this tiny group of the Ninety-Nine Percenters were able to live as One Percenters in an exclusive natural setting.

From my perch above this community, I could see myself joining this tight knit community and relaxing…but at another time.

The only ways to currently reach the homes in Shelter Cove is either by an arduous climb down or up multiple flights of stairs, hundreds by my count, with each landing bedecked by multiple *No Trespassing* signs that do not deter anyone with half the notion of wanting to visit the little inviting beach community, or via the ocean.

A single boat, landing quietly on the soft ocean sands, could easily let off a passenger unseen by the residents, who would then be free to wreak havoc on the community, or in my case, take out a potential target in the area, that being me.

No, with my back against the wall of San Pedro Mountain and just an ocean in front of me, there was absolutely no way out if I needed to make a quick escape, so Shelter Cove looked like it would be a final resting place for me if I followed Joe's advice.

16

FRIDAY MORNING, I GOT a call from Marilyn. The Feds had let her out. Cory had been true to his word on that account.

"Mike. I just got to my place. It's been torched."

"I know, we all got burned, all of our places. Where you staying?"

"I don't know. I guess with my dad. In the future, I don't know yet. The rents are too high right now. How 'bout you? Staying at Joe's?"

"Ahh, no. Don't want to be a burden and I can only do that for so long. Right now I'm staying at the Pacifica Beach Hotel, just for a little while. And like you said, the rents are just crazy right now."

"Mike, Mike, what's happening?" Marilyn implored for an answer, "Why did someone burn my apartment?"

"Revenge," I said. "Pure and simple. I guess Jasper and his cohorts didn't like what we did to them back on Market Street, and they wanted to get us back."

"Well, shit, they don't know who they're dealing with then. Do they Mike? They just opened up a can of whoop ass, and we ain't gonna stop until we get them good!"

"Yup," I said halfheartedly. I was still pretty numb about it all. "You hear from Ozzie?" I asked.

"No," Marilyn replied. "But just as I was being let out, I saw him talking to a couple of suits, and the funny thing was he was in a suit as well."

"Double crossers."

"What?" Marilyn asked.

"Feds," I said. "I worked to get you released, but I think they took Ozzie in return. I think maybe they're persuading him to work for them."

Marilyn pondered that for a moment, then replied, "Well good for him. It's probably a good job. Will pay well. It's what he was training for, right? From his college work?"

"Yeah," I agreed, but now I was down another body. "Listen," I said. "Have you been to your dad's place yet?"

"Not yet. I'm still just outside my apartment. Someone has sealed it. I think the police or firemen. I was thinking about calling someone or just going in."

"OK. I don't want you to go to your father's place yet. Marilyn, you are probably being watched, since you've just been to your apartment. Let's hook up and we'll figure out something for you. Right now, you need to stay somewhere public. Go over to Sloppy's. I'll be there shortly. We can talk things over a bit. OK?"

"OK," Marilyn whimpered.

"In about an hour, OK?"

"OK."

It took me a little over an hour to get to Sloppy's in San Francisco's Tenderloin district with all of the commuter traffic, but I found Marilyn was still on her way when I arrived. She had been dawdling after breaking into her apartment to retrieve some charred mementos.

"It's all gone. Everything ruined," she had cried on the phone when I called her to check in.

I knew how she was feeling, dazed and in a fog. When everything is taken away, you feel like a ghost. And I was still feeling that way, until I had a second cup of Sloppy's infamous coffee that was triggering acid reflux. I popped a couple of Tums and called Cory as I waited for Marilyn to arrive.

"Hey, Cory, it's Mike."

"Of course," Cory said. "So you got your girl back?"

"Yup," I said. "Now I want Ozzie."

"I don't have him," Cory said. "Some other department has him. To go over the downloads. He's a very smart fellow."

"I know."

"I think he'll get drafted."

"Shit," I said.

"Good for him," Cory responded. "Has quite a head on his shoulders. Well, him and his friends. I think he can do us some good over here. He kinda reminds me of myself when I was younger."

"He is nothing like you," I said dryly.

"OK. True," Cory said. "But nevertheless, I think he's found a new home."

"Shit," I repeated. "So anyway, any sightings of my step-brother?"

"Not yet. We're looking. Hey, I'm sorry, really sorry that your place got burned. We had a guy nearby, but he couldn't do anything."

"What do you mean you had a guy nearby."

"You don't think we wouldn't keep some eyes on you do you?"

I looked over my shoulder, scanned the patrons of Sloppy's, and looked out the restaurant's windows at the passersbys and the normal transients who parked themselves in doorways. There probably was someone watching me right then, but my senses had been dulled from lack of sleep and being beaten down. I just turned my attention back to my coffee cup.

"You had someone watching me and you let my place burn down."

"You've heard the police motto *To Protect and Serve* haven't you? Well in your case, we have our own motto, *To Subject and Observe*."

"What?"

"Mike, you are related to someone we really want to get our hands on, your brother Jasper. So just know that you will remain under the utmost scrutiny until he is captured. And also know that we will do our utmost to keep it from being known that we are watching you, as we do not wish to jeopardize any opportunity to get our hands on him. In that respect, when it was concluded that the attacks on your home, Joe's home, and your offices were being carried out by associates and not Jasper himself, our men held back."

"So you had people outside of my house, but did nothing."

"There was nothing to be gained."

"You let my house burn. You could have let me get killed."

"We called the fire department."

"So did everyone else!"

"Look, Mike, I know."

I didn't let Cory finish. I hung up and slammed the phone on the table. It rang again, from Cory, but I didn't pick up. I just sat and waited for Marilyn, who finally arrived some fifteen minutes later.

Marilyn was dirty, covered with soot from climbing around her burned out apartment. She looked a mess, tired, frazzled, and still wearing the same clothes that she had on when we had shot our way through Hoffman International Investments.

We hugged and she took a seat next to me in our booth. Normally I hate being crammed against a wall with someone sitting next to me in booth, but this time, it felt comforting.

We sat and ate and talked for a couple of hours, Marilyn telling of her experiences with the Feds, from when I last saw her to when she was released, to the finding that her apartment had been burned. I filled her in about everything I knew about Jasper, what Cory had told me about their interest in him, what Joe was thinking, that Ozzie was now probably working for the Feds, and about the night our homes and offices were attacked.

When we were both up to speed, Marilyn proclaimed, "I have one other update for you."

"Yes."

"When I got out, one of the first things I did was check my cell phone voicemail. And you remember Lyndon? Roosevelt Jones is his father, the one possible witness to Thomas Ballard's murder?"

I nodded that I remembered, and Marilyn continued, "Well, Lyndon said when he asked his dad if he knew anything about a murder back in the seventies in the Tenderloin, his dad just broke down and started crying. Told him not to get involved no matter, no how. Started asking Lyndon if he was being followed, who was asking. When Lyndon told him I had asked about it and how all that started, Roosevelt started asking about me, who I was, who my daddy is, and if we could be trusted."

"Sounds like he definitely knows something."

"Uh-huh!" Marilyn agreed.

"How old is Roosevelt? Do you know?"

"I think he's in his early eighties or nineties," Marilyn said. "He's still in that old folks home over by the Presidio. Lyndon said he's been having a hard time of late. Acting out with the nurses and all."

"Will Lyndon let you talk to Roosevelt directly?"

"I don't know," Marilyn said. "It might take a bit. Lyndon is very protective about his father now."

"Yeah, no doubt," I said. "With someone wanting to take a pot-shot at him, an ex-police captain, no less. Look, I thought this case was dead and done with, but with things the way they are, maybe following this lead will keep us, or at least you, occupied, and our minds off our current situation and what just happened. Look, my legs are beginning to cramp up from sitting here so long; do you have a place to stay? Staying at your father's place? Do you have any money to live off of?"

"I'm going to stay at a friend's place, I already called her. As for money…"

I emptied my wallet, two hundred, but I took Marilyn's phone. "The Fed's had this for a time," I advised. "It's probably bugged and tracked. Unless…maybe that is a good think. Someone watching over you."

"No eye that I want." Marilyn said. "Get rid of it."

We went our separate ways, parting with a hug and a kiss; Marilyn, to someplace in the Tenderloin, and me, out to the Pacifica Beach Hotel on California Highway One.

Early that evening, as I lay in my hotel room listening to the ocean, I suddenly felt a mixture of restlessness and dread overtake me. I pulled out the external hard drive, the one that Ozzie had given me that he said looked like the data was from a laptop, data that included a folder marked CSD. It was also the one item from our reverse hacking of Hoffman International Investments that I had failed to pass on to Cory. I had purchased a small black carrying case to protect it until I had a chance to go through it, document by document. But now wasn't the time. Paranoia was beginning to unnerve me and I felt a sudden urge to leave so I gathered up my few belongings, chased Poseidon down, forcing him into his kitty traveling box, and checked out of the hotel. One turn from the hotel and I was on Robert's Road, a stretch of Pacifica that I had taken many times to catch the sun as it set across the ocean. As always, it was beautiful, and this late evening promised to be spectacular when a promised full moon was to shine. I let Poseidon out of his carrier and he watched from a little nest of clothes I had made for him on the backseat.

After the last of the sun's rays had dropped behind the horizon, I drove over to Nick's Seafood Restaurant to pick up one of their world famous crab sandwiches to share with Poseidon. In their parking lot, we sat and ate as we watched the waves crash into the seawall and the moon rose behind us.

"How 'bout a couple of songs to end this wonderful evening?" I asked Poseidon, who responded to me with a blinking of his eyes.

We left Nick's and drove the couple of blocks to Vallamar Station. It was Friday night, now late enough for karaoke.

"Just a couple of quick songs," I assured Poseidon. "I'll be right back."

Karaoke at Vallamar Station was always my go-to if I was feeling blue and needed a pick-me-up, but this night, as soon as I opened the restaurant door, I knew tonight wouldn't be my night. I heard a familiar voice, Madame Gira, on the mike and she was singing "Witchy Woman."

Our eyes locked as soon as I entered the room. She smiled but continued singing, and I immediately had a flashback to that July night at the Surf Spot when we first met and she had said she saw "much turmoil in the lives of those around me. Lives and people changing. Things coming to light and not all of them will be for the best."

She had been right. Steve had sunk into the dark depths of the Tenderloin and Joe was in the process of retiring. All of us, the Coastside Detectives family, had lost their homes and livelihoods in one way or another. The only bright spots that I could see was Marilyn coming into her own and Ozzie, now off and on his own, making his own decisions and following his own path in life with the Feds.

I concluded it wasn't going to be my night so I left even before Madame Gira finished her song. I hopped back into my car, patted Poseidon, and promised just one last stop.

I drove for another ten minutes until we reached Mussel Rock out on the northern edge of Pacifica. I parked and grabbed a flashlight out of my glovebox and opened the chain link fence. There are a myriad of trails that one can take to where hang gliders land and take off of the nearby cliffs. There are also trails that take you down to a stretch of beach that runs from this tip of Pacifica all the way up to San Francisco's Ocean Beach and to the Cliff House in San Francisco.

I made my choice and took a trail that doubles back towards Pacifica and meanders along the Pacific Ocean shoreline. With the full moon lighting my path and the crashing waves, it was like a scene from an old movie.

After about a mile, the trail suddenly ended at a drop off into a rock-strewn cove where the opposing rock face revealed the continuation of the trail through a small tunnel. This tunnel, Tobin's Folly, was one of several tunnels built along the coast by the eccentric Hibernian Bank cofounder Richard Tobin. Richard Tobin had blasted his way through this serpentine block out by Muscle Rock back in 1874, just so he could take his horse and buggy from his Cliff House estate to his beach house near Pedro Point. He was an early version of the One Percenters, around just long enough to leave his own indelible mark on this earth.

I hiked down the trail through the rock filled cove. The rock being so slippery at times, I had to hold my small flashlight in my mouth just so I could scramble. At the base of the tunnel, Tobin's Folly, I paused to admire the entrance, hewed as it was through a block of dark green serpentine. It was impressive. Chisel marks made by hand could still be seen in the rock that was initially blasted to make this opening in the formidable coast.

I climbed up some boulders and cautiously made my way to the opposite end of the tunnel, wondering how long I had until the tide changed and trapped me inside. At the exit, I could see the ocean pounding the nearby stacks and beach, and far off in the distance, with the curve of the bay, I could see Rockaway Beach followed by the lights of Pacifica's Linda Mar district, where one of the offices of Coastside Detective's once stood.

At that moment, I realized it would be the last time I set my eyes on the town for quite a long time. I took both my and Marilyn's cell phones and left them at the entrance of the cave.

The dream that I once had, and that had become my life in Pacifica, had ended.

A HINT OF THINGS TO COME

BOOK V

BOOK V

COASTSIDE
DETECTIVES
FOUNDATIONS

By Matthew F. O'Malley

IT HAD BEEN A little over two years since I left Pacifica, chased away by my nemesis, my half-brother Jasper, and my own paranoia, and it was nearly as long since I had last seen Joe Ballard, my former partner in the Coastside Detectives Agency, in person. So as a trio of caffeine crooners played and sang at the Chit-Chat Café in the Manor District of Pacifica, we spent a good portion of our initial meeting time going over the changes to the world and the town of Pacifica since I left.

In the larger world, Vladimir Putin worked on rebuilding the Soviet Union, flexing his country's muscles as much as he like to flex his own, China made inroads into making itself a military power, creating or claiming islands as their own to the chagrin of Japan, Vietnam, the Philippines and South Korea, while a young little fat man in North Korea began to stamp his feet and proclaim that he would be the end of the United States.

In the United States, it was revealed that the National Security Agency, NSA, was spying not only on terrorists and enemies of the

United States, but on friends and Americans as well, tapping directly into transatlantic fiber optic cables for raw Internet data, as well as the servers of large companies including Google, Apple, Facebook, and Microsoft. It was also revealed the agency had the ability to access a wide range of information stored on smartphones and could even listen in on conversations when it was thought a phone had been turned off.

These national security measures did nothing, however, to completely squash any terrorist attacks. In Boston, two disenfranchised and delusional immigrants set off bombs at the Boston Marathon and later, a radicalized Islamic married couple in San Bernardino carried off, at the time, the deadliest terrorist attack on American soil since September 11, 2001.

As we discussed these events, the music in the Chit Chat Café continued and our conversations moved to more local changes; the opening of the Devil's Slide tunnel, the building of multimillion dollar homes off of Fassler Avenue, and the closing of Kerri's coffee shop. This closing of Kerri's, which had been at the Linda Mar mall for over forty years, was followed with the closing of the Denny's Restaurant a couple of doors down from our old Coastside Detectives agency location. For Joe, this was a double whammy and he didn't feel he had a local place to go for breakfast.

"There's a new shop in Kerri's spot, just haven't given it a shot yet."

From our window seat at the Chit Chat Cafe, I could see my Ford Escape parked across the street and along a stretch of Pacific Ocean bluffs. An elderly man walking along the side of the road paused to tie his shoes near my car. For a moment, I tried to remember if I had locked my door. I didn't want to startle the man, so I decided to wait for him to move further along before I used my remote lock.

As I waited for the man to continue on his way, I looked far beyond my car and into the Pacific where a small pod of grey whales breached and spouted. I pointed the whales out to Joe and he remarked on the clarity of the day and how we could easily see the Farallon Islands.

"You know," Joe said, "I think I know what Jasper was looking for, out in the ocean, out by those islands."

I heard Joe, but it didn't sink in what he was talking about as my mind was busy, soaking in the gorgeous day outside. It was turning out to be a sunny day with a clear blue sky.

"This is a beautiful part of the world." I said.

"Who has it better than us?' Joe asked.

"Nobody." I replied, pressing the door lock button on my remote.

That was when my car exploded.

Printed in the United States
By Bookmasters